ULTRAMARINE

# *Ultramarine*

# Mariette Navarro

### translated from the French
### by Eve Hill-Agnus

DEEP VELLUM PUBLISHING

DALLAS, TEXAS

Deep Vellum Publishing
3000 Commerce St., Dallas, Texas 75226
deepvellum.org · @deepvellum

Deep Vellum is a 501c3 nonprofit literary arts organization
founded in 2013 with the mission to bring
the world into conversation through literature.

Text copyright © 2021 Mariette Navarro
Translation copyright © 2025 by Eve Hill-Agnus
Originally published as *Ultramarins* by Quidam (Meudon, France, 2021)

FIRST ENGLISH EDITION, 2025

Support for this publication has been provided in part by the National Endowment for the
Arts, the Texas Commission on the Arts, the City of Dallas Office of Arts and Culture, the
Communities Foundation of Texas, and the Addy Foundation.

This work received support for excellence in publication and translation from Albertine
Translation, formerly Hemingway Grants, a program created by Villa Albertine.

ISBNs: 978-1-64605-357-5 (paperback) | 978-1-64605-369-8 (ebook)

LIBRARY OF CONGRESS CATALOGING-IN-PUBLICATION DATA

Names: Navarro, Mariette, author. | Hill-Agnus, Eve, translator.
Title: Ultramarine / Mariette Navarro ; translated from the French by Eve
Hill-Agnus.
Other titles: Ultramarins. English
Description: Dallas, Texas : Deep Vellum, 2025.
Identifiers: LCCN 2024033021 (print) | LCCN 2024033022 (ebook) | ISBN
9781646053575 (trade paperback) | ISBN 9781646053698 (ebook)
Subjects: LCGFT: Thrillers (Fiction) | Psychological fiction. | Sea
fiction. | Novels.
Classification: LCC PQ2714.A93 U5813 2025 (print) | LCC PQ2714.A93
(ebook) | DDC 843/.92--dc23/eng/20240725
LC record available at https://lccn.loc.gov/2024033021
LC ebook record available at https://lccn.loc.gov/2024033022

Cover Design by Daniel Benneworth-Gray
Interior Layout and Typesetting by KGT

PRINTED IN CANADA

# CONTENTS

There are the living, the dead, and sailors.

They already know, intimately, to which category they belong. There are no real surprises, no real revelations. They know, wherever they may be, if they belong or if they do not.

There are the living, busy building, and the dead, calm in their hollow tombs.

And there are sailors.

# I

A space slipped into even the most mundane gestures, the gestures of work repeated each day. A tiny blank space that hadn't existed before—a hovering second. And in this hovering second, this vague, suspended second, the rest of life rushed in, took its ease, unfurled its consequences.

She is distinctly aware of this, as it's in her body that the tiny gap found a path. She has no medical explanation to offer, could not even say whether this slow breeze traversing her is serious, regrettable, enemy. A draft against which she must tighten her muscles a little more firmly.

She doesn't know if the weakness preceded the decision, or if everything happened all at once when, at the end of a meal, she said, "Alright." She doesn't know if the desire

9

to give in was already lodging within her or if someone in the crew, by a word or a look, broke through her necessary coolness. She believes that now her insides are more porous to the ocean winds.

She hears herself say "alright" in a voice that isn't quite her own, not her work voice, her captain's voice. It's a shriller sound, out of place. She, who is always so careful about this, notices as she says the word that it has not had time to come from her stomach. It was born directly in her throat and hatched publicly: "Alright." So, if her voice has spoken, she can only follow, as she is not in the habit of disagreeing with herself. Until now, there has never been a gap between her thoughts and her words.

As she is calm and self-assured, she lets herself be led by this gamine's voice that tumbles out in the middle of a meal. She clears her throat and repeats in her commander's voice, with the full weight of her authority: "Alright."

It's not just inside of her that the breath drifts. For several days now, she has heard the rumors, the stifled laughter. She let herself be surprised by the expansive mood of a crew she thought she knew well, a crew she'd recruited for its reliability and the seriousness upon which she depends.

As always before embarking, she did everything she could to balance the various temperaments of the sailors who would accompany her. A dosage made with a chemist's rigor, whereas she is more mechanically inclined.

Before each departure, she knows she is taking on the risks of the reaction's inevitable precipitate—the hot blood after several weeks of cohabitation, the neglected rancor, the sadness that lives in liquor, the desire to end it all, the too-long nights, the bodies that buckle under the weight of solitude. But she hadn't anticipated the sudden friendship, the joy of being accomplices. She's disoriented enough to be uncertain if she should take part in it. Hence her strange smile and her voice that has risen an octave.

Ultimately, she accepted that they were speaking louder and laughing more, their gazes seeking out one another's approval for a word just spoken. As always, she made sure that the bursts of laughter were dealt out evenly among them, that no one was forgotten in the distribution of levity, no member of the crew the unwitting object of the others' joviality. She even let herself brush against a shoulder. A few days more and she might almost have embraced one of them in the moonlight.

—

She's been a captain for many years: three now on this ship, with new crews hired regularly and months on shore between one cargo and the next—that other life that she forgets almost as soon as she boards the ship, as soon as she stows her bag in her cabin. The going is easy on this route, especially at this time of year. Adventure was for the reading she did as a schoolgirl; now it's for the tales she invents at parties on land, when others manage to get her to talk about herself. She has known most of the officers since their school days, and they work in tandem without having to say very much.

She's a ship captain's daughter and there was never any question of her choosing a life on land: from the start she had learned too much about ships to turn away from the sea. She belongs to water the way others are proud of their distant origins. There was never any reason to break with or reject it. She chose navigation, this quintessentially human knowledge; she chose ancient artisanship and modern machines, numbers and sensations, cosmic abstractions and the sun on her face. And all of this gave her a certain maturity and density.

She observed the work of others, of the men who'd come before her. She learned all there was to learn and proved herself under their exacting eyes, the sometimes condescending, wary gazes. She skipped no steps; she is a stranger to the idea of privilege, to anything but the patient respect of procedures. She discovered that the work—that reassuring expanse of physical labor—soothed her. With seriousness and against all odds, she won her authority.

During her first crossing, she hardly slept: she was everywhere at once, wanted to know everything. She would, in an instant, have taken on any crew member's duties. Whenever she turned her back, they smiled; they didn't think her career or health would last long. They said she would get over it, her appetite for men's work, that someone would manage to keep her on land, in a house, captain over a woman's sphere; they said that she didn't have strong arms or the right hormones for the long run. Only once did she ever make a fist to fight. She would have had the advantage, too, if the tension hadn't been defused right away, if someone hadn't placed a hand on her shoulder. Now that she's the one to give orders and determine the arc of others' careers, no one pipes up anymore. The feminine has threaded a path in their minds, entered their stories just like famous sailors' nicknames.

Little by little, the weather became for her a sense sharper than the others; precise cartography, too, with its little crosses traced every twenty minutes on the large map in her office, marking their position. With each new crossing, she is unsurprised to see herself moving south, moving toward fairer skies and skirting atmospheric depressions, avoiding them as best she can. She has learned how oily expanses spread, the soft envelopment of green foam.

She loves looking at maps, knows them by heart, annotates them, sorts them. She knew them all before she ever set sail. The beauty of their colors. Sometimes she grows tired of the overly rational route they've taken between two points: she craves slowness. So she gives an order to slow the engines, intentionally losing an hour or two as they approach the nearest land.

Many have sought to sail with her in recent years. They know that all will be orderly, that the human machine will work as well as the blazing engine, that they'll be able to settle into a crossing without storms. They like the calm she radiates and, without admitting it, they're relieved to be under her protection. She prefers tight crews—one or two loyal officers, not too chatty. When it comes to deciding who she wants on board, she chooses the gruff men, the shy ones.

She returned to the sea a month ago, replacing a colleague about to retire and happy to give him the longest periods on land: Christmases, summers, school holidays. She takes on any job, fetches the cargo ship wherever it may be, takes charge of the inventory, makes up for delays. She's had the feeling of late that she is sailing on velvet, that she's found in her work the fluidity of a perfectly executed dance. When she closes her eyes, the freighter is her own body, stable and straight. So much so that she forgets the waves.

Her cabin is the most spacious one. With a large desk. It's the quietest, too, even if sailors regularly come by to inform her of a delay, a weather alert, an incident among the crew members.

She has gotten used to having an answer for everything. A voice adapted to each circumstance. A mask to hide every impatience. With each new crossing, she has to find her bearings again, introduce herself to the crew and to the passengers if there are any. She detects the fears, the first-timers at sea, senses who she'll lean on and the jealousies she'll have to defuse.

She doesn't shake hands. She touches only metal, or

the fabric of her own clothing when she crosses her arms over her chest. She ties her hair back just above the nape of her neck, and it falls straight to the middle of her back. When she moves, it doesn't sway: she keeps it in place, another straight line among all the straight lines of her body.

She never locks her cabin; she must be ready at the slightest shudder, the least alert. She sleeps with her clothes on. She hears the rough breathing of the men on the other side of the wall. She sleeps very little anyway. When she rests, it's only to obey the rules. Often, it's in her chair that she lets herself close her eyelids, lets herself go to the swaying of the ship.

Most of her time she spends above deck. At the center of the bridge. In the seat reserved for her. She wants to see with her own eyes before receiving the placid confirmation of the devices. She loves the intimacy of this spot—the calm and the concentration. For the last few trips, a Romanian helmsman has been working at her side. He knows only enough French to read off measurements and use technical words, which he does his best to pronounce. She doesn't ask him any questions, is content to watch him when it isn't her turn to survey the horizon. He's very young. Like most of the sailors aboard the freighter. She doesn't know what pushed him toward the sea, he or any of the others—what pushed him into a job so foreign, so far from his nature that even after several years he still vomits when the waves surge, and sometimes, when facing the ocean, his gaze suddenly empties and he panics. Perhaps it was the salary, or a thirst. Though it's she who drinks a glass of wine each night, always at the same time. More than anything, she loves it when gusts of rain sweep against the windows at that exact moment. Then she unties her hair, frees her skull. The officers are there, but for an instant, she relaxes her shoulders and face.

When, during that dinner, after four days at sea, her chief mate leans toward her and, with a candor she doesn't recognize in him, asks, "Could we, really—no kidding—cut the engines, lower the lifeboats, and treat ourselves to a little swim?" a voice tumbles out of her and she says, without thinking, "Alright." Repeats, "Alright." A brief silence follows, of course, and then a great, incredulous laugh.

## II

First, they trace a circle so as to be its center. A large circle that encompasses everything: the blue, its black masses, its white flecks. Bounded by nothing but the now-round horizon.

From the ship, they trace a circle with their eyes.

They hope for silence.

Their gazes get lost in the curve that surrounds them.

They hope for abstraction. They make of this blue circle a rigid cloth, a ground on which to take their first steps. They squint, maintaining this illusion until a wave appears, a lapping that once again renders everything liquid, deep.

They trace a circle on the surface, and it's as though they took the sea to be paper, their arms to be their childhood compasses. They don't ask themselves what's below: they only seek the perfection of the circle and to dive into its center. They imagine the concentric waves their tiny human bodies will produce. They believe that they can plunge into a mirror without being engulfed by the swell, that they can disappear to the side of the world where light no longer shines.

They hope for silence when they cut the engines—save for the play of water, its slapping against the hull, the revenge of the wind once the engines are still. From then on, any creaking and sighing will be brought on only by mechanical forces, by gusts of wind, the ocean's billows, the wave-tossed steel and the men's breathing in response to these great hisses.

When the engines stop, the men lose the balance they've finally managed to gain: they regress in their learning. They're once again crazed dogs crashing into things, vomiting out their intestines. And still they feel a kind of euphoria to have come to this point.

They all leave their cabins at the appointed time, are faithful to the rendezvous, not one has so much as imagined letting the others down. They've been freed of nothing, of course, least of all worry. They look anxiously for the slightest anomaly, a sagging or crack in the chosen din-ghy, a leak, perhaps—unsure that they'll be able to detect danger when it arises. They're stripped of their reflexes. To distract themselves, they turn this din drained of all famil-iarity into a kind of music.

When everything stops, they are left with neither a trade nor a planned course. They don't know much once they've left the instrument panel behind. Barefoot along the gangway, they become tremulous; but they like the way the sun burns their skin. So begins the work of feeling.

They struggle to keep from slipping while making fun of themselves, turn their unsteadiness into a new game. Amid the ship's rocking, they follow one another without a word, placing their hands on the cold guardrails to reassure themselves: a known sensation. They laugh a little at the sin-gle tremor that begins to run through them all, identical.

Moving along the deck toward one of the lifeboats, they measure their own folly, wondering if this is really called for, and still they go through with the motions they've agreed upon: unfold the ladders, grab hold of the rigging, become aware of newly found muscles in their tensed arms. Prepare to descend toward the sea.

They lean over and peer down, assess the ten or so

meters that stand between them and the water. For the moment, the metal gangway is still a piece of land on which they can walk with dry feet. Glancing up, they double-check for the expected fair weather, and gradually take comfort in a purely turquoise reflection.

Passing the Azores was the signal, the last contact with land. They waited to be out of sight of any coast, of any ship engaged in its business. They disconnected the radar. From here, no bird could bring news of their presence.

They sit side by side in one of the lifeboats. They no longer question the path from idea to action, now that they've reached this perfect region of calm water, the same one they've evoked these last few nights on deck under the glow of the moon. They're amazed to think of the promises they made each other so lightly, but now they let themselves descend to the water, until a light bump from beneath tells them they're there. Mere centimeters from the surface, all they have to do is swing their legs overboard. Everything, now, can begin.

*Abyssal plain.* They remember this name on the map, this union of words, poetic and terrifying, that made them imagine the ocean floor would suck them into those darkest of fathoms. They thought of those who go diving there and dream of walking on this floor, a feat rarer than walking on the moon.

They themselves only have memories of swimming at the beach: carefully entering at the edge of waves, a supervised resort, proper bathing suits, the sluggishness and slight sickness that comes of sleeping in the heat of the day. Or perhaps they remember rivers, feet encountering pebbles and their attempts to keep their balance despite the cutting sensation.

So, two feet plunge into nothingness, and the whole body follows.

On the commander's bridge, up above, fingers tapped binoculars and a few deep breaths were taken. Not a word before going outside, as the least sound would be recorded. The ship's position was checked, and before it was turned off, the radar confirmed that no vessel was approaching the cargo ship. A cigarette was smoked at the first sensation of swaying—a sign of nervousness, or of exultation.

From the bridge, they halted the momentum, fastened

the ship at the center of the circle of cloth and made, from the tons of metal, a dead butterfly, pinned, magnificent.

So they start there. In suspension. For the very first time, they put both feet into the ocean. Slide into the water. Thousands of kilometers from any beach.

No one will ever know, but it's now that they're born, out of the air and into the water, willing exiles from their vertical condition and their age. In the space of a second, they invert the order of things: maybe somewhere, birds take flight backward or a river suddenly returns to its source. This is what they sense, haphazardly, and each in his own language.

As births go, under the perfect arc of the horizon, it's much more successful than the first time, between a hospital's square walls, twenty, thirty, forty years ago, somewhere in Europe. They are born adults and of their own free will, feet forward, arms tucked along their flanks, and in their throats a barely held-back song, the beginning of a cry.

## III

They slide into the water.

Tips of toes then whole bodies. Ache of the cold and of salt that burns as if it became more painful on skin contact. Ribcages compressed by the immense weight of the ocean: it seems as though the enormous mass, gray in places, doesn't let itself be pierced so easily. Just see how, since their departure, the ocean has systematically sealed the water behind the freighter that, on the contrary, puts all its strength into splitting the surface. You don't tear the ocean like fabric or leave an imprint as you would in sand or snow. Plunging in, you condemn yourself to invisibility.

As they slide in, they wonder if they're all able to feel the same thing, if the ocean can play that role, too—of tying souls together when bodies frolic in it, of transmitting sensations like a bolt of lightning. As they touch the water, they form a team in exaltation: this current they feel they spark with each movement could almost shine light on the ocean depths.

They have no desire for bravura, no sense of the hour to come. It seems they need the first slap of water to make their journey to the present. They have nothing particular in mind. They'll see what motions come first to help them float as well as they can, to help them get their bearings in the circle now deformed by their swimming. They'll see if breath will follow, if silence will paralyze them, if their euphoria, here, will stand in for fins.

To each his secret image of freedom, to each his own shock as he changes elements. Landscapes scroll past under their eyelids: childhood vacations, plains so vast they seem prehistoric, diluvian rains, bicycles picking up speed under a beating sun, tiny houses hidden among boulders, fields of sunflowers and fields of rapeseed, beaches, spices, cabins.

To witness them is to see faces ecstatic and abandoned, bodies arched with pleasure. And each one knows that it's in his own language that the sea is the sea and the ocean, powerful.

25

—

They can see what each man is made of by the way he enters the water—the bruises under the skin, the forgotten bumps, the sore backs. It's easy to recognize supple youth or tired muscles, flesh that's been loved and caressed and bodies that have been too long forsaken. Not everyone will trace precisely the same aperture on the surface: all do not carry the same weight.

But they slide in without a splash, without stirring up more water than is necessary: scarcely any foam forms around their thighs as their legs churn. In a second, they are underwater, their hair jellyfish, finally exposed to something other than ocean spray. It undulates, utterly weightless, freeing their skulls from pressure.

The water in their ears sounds like an unknown hum. They dive one or two meters deep, hear their hearts beating in their temples, grasp another kind of silence. They've left the sounds of the earth and of the surface: they discover the music of their own blood, a drumming to the point of jubilation, percussion that could lead them to a trance. Dark sound of held breaths, symphony of lightness.

They made a point of nudity, and now it seems that this is what preceded the idea for the swim: a desire to be naked in the water—a desire stupid and precise enough to become their obsession. Above all else, a desire of the skin, skin pushing toward madness, skin seeking lightness and bracing coolness.

The skin now rises up, feasts on cold, on salt, on the rhythmic tossing of even the most minor waves. In the first minute they evolve underwater, making star shapes with their bodies and kicking, losing their bearings, but opening their eyes in the sea to look for the freighter—that large shadow, the gigantic hull—then forgetting what they were looking for when the sun glints on the surface and they slowly approach it with their faces, emerge and breathe.

As they slid in, each man took up his own space, recreated his own circle. Caught up in the euphoria, they are no longer cautious: they measure only the distance between their head and their feet, only the sensation of lengthening. Utterly consumed as they are by the pleasures of drifting, they no longer know how to count using any terrestrial or navigational measurements. They talk and sing without listening to one another. They drift farther and farther apart.

For the first ten minutes, they have no particular intention. They slide into the water and move in chaotic ways, swimming their invented strokes around the lifeboat. They do the breaststroke underwater, then emerge breathing hard. They're fully in their bodies. The dark water becomes transparent when they dive. They have a new energy, from where they don't know: they want to try everything, see everything, live everything. Their clocks have been wound back to the start, and they shout with full lungs to make sure. They explore nothing but their own flesh plunged into this liquid, discover their own resistance to the currents of this deeply calm ocean. Never mind that the horizon tilts as their heads bob on the water's surface. One after another, the waves hide them from the ship's view. They feel, all of a sudden, what it means to mean nothing. A little salt blinds them, a bit of transparency mesmerizes them, and then this color they've never seen before: the color of green eyes.

They marvel at the smallest shiny object, even if it's merely their own thigh reflecting light. They understand that these will be the purest seconds, with nothing to frighten them, no shadow or cloud. They draw out the instant, each tracing his own path in the water. They do the crawl in long, leisurely strokes and know that these will be immortal minutes, perhaps the only ones like this for a long time—the only ones during which they won't wonder about the return journey but instead carve their furrow straight ahead with perfect poise.

In the eleventh minute, they ease up on their movements and let the cold seize them. They breathe. With their heads above water, they see the sky differently, perhaps closer, or of a deeper blue, or perhaps their eyes are simply tired from the sun. They straighten up, realize they've lost their bearings. They don't know how to hold their bodies perpendicular to the water, since the ocean mischievously twists itself. Is it the sun playing tricks on them, or have the waves picked up slightly? The men laugh to themselves again, test the echo in the chamber of their skulls, measure the strange distance between the first questions that come to their mind and the sound of their voices, between the water's din and the others' silence.

They no longer know if it's their arms slicing through the water or the water clutching their arms. No longer know if they're free to choose their path or if the lifeboat is drawing away. They continue their exploration, amused as they thrust one leg up into the foam. They are the swells' playthings, their voluntary toys. They cooperate with the wind that ripples the surface and heightens their trepidation.

The fear of storms belongs to another time, other sailors. Today, everything is under control—their health, the weather, their journeys, and even their foolishness: under control.

They have no trouble staying above water. Nothing worries them yet. They are men familiar with their bodies, with training sessions, men attuned to their every weakness.

They're not easily intimidated, not men made vulnerable in a moment of distraction. They tell themselves they've known other times in life when they needed to be fully present, concentrated, centered. They know they chose this career precisely for these moments of struggle between themselves and nature. So they crane their necks as far as they can and try to make out where the others are swimming. They know that exactly now is when it's important to encourage the others and to be encouraged, to bring back the group and support one another.

They're a team and grown-up men, after all, even if in the water, for a moment, they thought they weighed the same as they did at ten years old.

They look for the lifeboat and easily spot it twenty or so meters away, flamboyant and orange, swaying like a signal.

But are they dreaming or is no one on board? And no one swimming around it, either? They blink several times—the salt may be blinding them. Gently they mock themselves for their sudden childish uncertainty.

Searching around them, their necks like periscopes, they enlarge the field of research. They don't know how fast the others are swimming or what direction each has taken. But try as they may to crane their necks, to swivel their heads in every direction, there is no one: emptiness across the whole blue cloth, nothing but the neon raft that sways and, farther away still, the looming freighter.

And so doubt sets in, a sudden absence of all logic. They laugh to prove their presence, at least to themselves. They conjure elaborate scenarios in which they're dreaming and the others have evaporated, imagine they've been pranked or struck with near-sightedness. They question their grasp of time: after all, their joy may have kept them out longer than the others; maybe they don't know their own physical strength and the minutes they spent splashing around were in fact hours. Yes, surely their crewmates clambered on board long ago by way of the orange lifeboat while they weren't paying attention, and then sent the raft back toward the solitary swimmer, the happy paddler. But try as they may to parse the logic, to look around for clues, they know they're fooling themselves. They weren't expecting this dizziness, this quite sudden failure of all of their faculties. They were caught up in the wonder.

In the twentieth minute, they have no choice but to marshal their thoughts onto something concrete. They remember the ladders and buoys, that the lifeboat is bobbing nearby, and that, whatever happens, they're watched from above, on the ship's deck. They go over the chain of actions and consequences in their head. They remember not to fear anything, neither the ocean's depths nor the freighter's height. They offer themselves proof of life: they stretch, breathe, spit and shiver, utter a few intimate truths out loud to themselves as well as grand metaphysical sentences. Those who don't manage to solve the question of their immediate future through logic try humor instead, then tire of their mute monologue altogether: shut up and swim.

But, for some, it's too late. They've thought clearly of the kilometers beneath their feet and encountered what they weren't expecting to meet here—vertigo. There's no difference any longer between bodies suspended over bridges and parapets, bodies that climb mountains seeking the void, and their own bodies, here and now, their innocent bathers' bodies. There's no longer any difference between the excruciating stages of a suicide attempt and their prudent swimming around the lifeboat. The thought has opened up under their feet and there is a wrenching in their stomachs.

Some—and it only took one second—can no longer look at the water, imagine its shadowy depths, raise their bodies to flutter their feet: they plummet from all possible buildings, from every cliff, from every nightmare.

Others, in their heads, have joined the chorus of the drowned fallen from a ship's deck in the middle of a storm. They've become the assassinated, condemned to the black of night. They're the shipwrecked whose ship has split in two and left them here in their incapacity, more laughable than driftwood. From what century and in what dead language are the voices they begin to hear? And so they swim desperately.

A half hour: long enough to experience time at a standstill, their heart beating in their throat, the cry from within that suffocates laughter. They feel, keenly, their vanishing and their ignorance.

There are some who heard nothing but their own breath. Who quickly dismissed the thought of an animal,

33

of some unexpected contact as they stretched out their legs. They shut out the probability of a jellyfish, a stingray, a shark. The most stable ones let themselves be comforted by the memory of things they've read, by sets of numbers and probabilities. But now they all retrace their path, hoping they're not wrong about the whereabouts of the lifeboat.

They won't have cast a very large net in the middle of the ocean.

They won't have swum more than thirty-five minutes.

They won't have been anything other than land dwellers, panicking in the deep blue.

They will have seen their lives summed up in a wave and hoped for shore and an awakening.

## IV

There are the living, the dead, and sailors.

You can still be breathing and already be dead. You can be discreet and terribly alive. You can carry the ocean within you, having never smelled the odor of salt, having never even left the countryside or the city.

You know whether you're dead or a sailor, even stuck on land. You know when you're drifting, when you're just passing by. When the ground isn't solid under your feet. You know when you're from a place without really being so, always summoned by the next departure.

There are sailors, some of whom have never seen the sea and who would never call themselves by this name they don't even know. They share some quality with the dead, even when you're talking to them, even when you're pulling them toward life to ward off their despair, even as you touch them and extract promises from them.

There are sailors, so absent as to cause vertigo, who befriend death without crossing its border, haunted by questioning to the point of gauntness, no longer here in any event, drifting with their feet planted, with this enviable power to look from afar at how life is getting along without them.

She could say of all the people she's met in life what they are and what awaits them: wandering or anchoring down, home or perpetual departure, verticality or the infinite horizon.

It makes no difference, but it's her way of reading the world.

As for her, she belongs to the sea. Well before she ever set sail, in the terrestrial years of a warm home and sibling-hood, a mother's lap and the daily route to school, even in the years of a city far from any harbor, of academic studies and the books she read, she didn't tread the same ground as others, though this did not in the least prevent love and astonishment, racing in the grass and stealing kisses on benches. She was just more prone to disappearing, to flying away at the slightest draft.

This last time on land was the most striking. She had stayed several months, taken care of all sorts of things, met all sorts of people, rekindled a few old friendships, pursued a romantic fling that she then didn't know what to do about. All *attachment* of course was impossible; she was tired of explaining this again and again.

The last few weeks before her departure, she was certain that the city couldn't tolerate her any longer, that she was the superfluous element amid the interlocking buildings and bodies. She moved forward as though instinctively sensing unseen violence and electric fences. For months, she had no longer thought of strolling the streets; she didn't have time—in the silence of an apartment never properly furnished, she only awaited boarding.

She knows each time how the unsettled city will push her to its edge again in a simple slipping, always toward the outside, to the bustle of the shipyard, the kilometers of feverishness and stacked sheet metal, the docks, their pale arms, the breathless boats, pierced by she knows not what wounds. She knows the feeling of arriving at port, of being crushed by a shadow, frightened by scrap metal. The whole horizon is suddenly blocked by a looming mass. Things no longer fit into any frame. She loves that moment, on her boat's threshold, when, for an instant, she doesn't know which are the right proportions, what is the true scale of values.

She reminds herself that the harbor is hostile: it's where one meets machines more limber and faster than oneself, machines that steam ahead unbothered by any presence, moving aside obstacles with great siren calls. A zone reserved for giant insects. This is what she calls them, but they are ten-meter-tall forklifts that have total control over her life. One could say it's the price to pay for leaving the city and approaching the water.

Even the edge now is dangerous, sharp as a blade. Every time, she has to get used to it: the earth is no longer her playground. Go on, quick, so that the boat can set off. Free itself from the bank and its knife-edge.

She belongs to the water and knows her trade. Though no trip ever begins with certainty. She has to ask herself, every time, what possessed her to take to the sea, this accursed appetite for rupture, when she knows that it's far more comfortable to watch one's life go by between four walls than to bear this damned difference of hers—the living, the dead, and she, the captain—with the tingling in her legs, which she entrusts, like an idiot, to the sea.

To begin with, after the first few days aboard, a sort of mutation happens between flesh and metal, just as it's said that plastic melds with fish at the bottom of the ocean. That's what she thinks sometimes. A very slight evolution of the species. A return to the sea's depths.

There is, first of all, a change in the composition of her skin's smell, the smell of her hands: a mix of grease and scrap metal, an ointment. What happens is chemical as much as mechanical. So she gives herself over to this stinking life, to diesel, the black blood of the animal that bears her on its back—this animal at once dead and alive, spitting like a human when it accelerates, howling when there's phlegm rattling in its airways.

In the beginning, she feels like everything is topsy-turvy— that her organs are setting sail without her, that they are the ones taking to the sea, seeking to escape. Without her. Because for several days she is clumsy. Because in the beginning she doesn't know how to do anything anymore and wherever she goes, her body comes up against a barrier, a stairway, a rule, a guardrail, a new door, a danger, a gust of wind, a furnace, a ramp, a hesitation, a panel, a parapet, a spurt of water, an optical illusion, rain, an alarm, a vibration, a ladder, a doubt, a timetable, a change in temperature, a radar, a safety regulation, a drowsiness, a voice, a fire alarm, a total powerlessness. The bruises are part of the transformation.

She remembers that it's never easy. That you don't go from one category to another, as if from death to life, without losing some of your bearings and flexibility. She knows you're not always welcome on the ocean's back, that you can't cling to its mane with impunity.

Something too big enters her field of vision and takes up all the room inside of her. Makes itself at home in the two hemispheres of her brain. Something jostles, oppresses, and frees at the same time, as it slides between her organs. She can't say whether the alloy between her body and the scrap metal is a protection, an insect's shell just under her skin, an immense shield, or a lever meant to make her insides fluid, to denature her.

After a while, she accepts the transformation and lets herself be changed, a little.

# V

Now, on the bridge, she watches for the emergence of a ship that might be troubled by their motionlessness. She knows that anything could sound the alarm: all it would take is a minute too long with the radar turned off; all it would take is a call gone unanswered for a procedure to start in an office tower somewhere that would make an earth-dweller's adrenaline rise. All it would take is being located by an airplane. There would then be the little bell that calls humans to order, the helicopters at the ready to tear themselves away from the nearest land. Nothing is far at engine-speed. With or without wind, all it would take is a few hours for expert hands to reach them, to correct the course of her deviance. She knows it's impossible to disappear completely, that illusion one gets from cutting the channels enough time for a swim. So she observes the glassy water and reconnects with the feeling, this slight slowing of her movements, this subtle resistance to common sense. She hasn't forgotten her sailors. She goes out portside, to the side where the lifeboat was unhooked. She has to lean over, rocking her chest forward to see it.

She locates the men in the water, next to the orange lifeboat. From up here, she doesn't recognize any of them. She could pick up the binoculars, but, again, no: the slight hovering is there, holding back her movements. With her naked eye, she lets herself take in the spectacle of compositions they draw, small thrashing dots studding the blue circle. In this bank of humans swimming, she tries to find a logic or an organizing principle, like when she makes out faces in the craggy coasts of the islands she approaches, or secret formulas in the long calculations of navigation. Alone, for hours, she dives into them as a challenge sometimes, a race against the electronic instruments.

She contemplates these twenty men who go where they will, where they can, however they can, because they've decided to, because all of a sudden their mission no longer mattered, nor their learned trade itself. An idea flitted through their bodies: they wanted to be naked. They

43

no longer feared being monitored or evaluated, or causing a delay with quantifiable consequences. She sees these men, naked in the water because they stopped thinking about safety or limits. They're like children happy in their little tub, in their swimming pool, who don't ask themselves whether or not they can swim. She watches these men risk drowning because something inside of her said *alright.*

So, the new space just below her heart is similar to their clumsy dive. No need to throw herself into the water along with them to feel their vertigo. She knows she'll have to expect this from today onward: a bite's wound, a violent rejection of all straight lines.

Her eyes are growing tired. The sun is high. She tells herself that they should at least do something while she's watching them, a race, a synchronized dance, a wave in her direction or some kind of collective disappearing act. Without their clothing, she can no longer tell who is who, but she seems to hear the sound of their bodies hitting the water, the echo that their boys' breathing makes, the words they exchange to sound courageous. Though they are, after all, but tiny creatures, far less agile than the flying fish whose schools they cleave at full speed, fish that break away, leaping to either side of the ship.

With the binoculars, she chooses one of them at random, one of these naked men who breathes and stretches the arms he uses so rarely this way, a man transcending his condition for no reason, for bragging rights or out of a magnificent urge. Happy to have rediscovered his crawl stroke, he doesn't turn back toward the freighter, seems to have forgotten all danger, all distances, latitudes, longitudes, and disappearances at sea. She thinks she might recognize one of the sailors with whom she has exchanged only a few words since the beginning of the trip—useful and measured words, in the only language they share, that of work. When he stops swimming she can hardly see his face anymore, but it seems to her that he is speaking or shouting and won't stop endlessly soliloquizing, as though suddenly inhabited by a poem.

She focuses in on them, one by one. She would like to know what they're saying to each other, eyes closed, necks stretched toward the sky. Baby birds, she thinks, fallen from the nest and squawking as best they can to practice their language, not having learned to fly. Some swim the backstroke, others the crawl, nearly leaving her field of vision.

When she manages to make out a face clearly through the lenses, she concentrates on the lips' movements to see if it looks like a known language or a song. She worries a little that there might be a message in need of decoding, a call for help she would need to grasp in order to act. But what could she do then, except wave her arms wildly, yelling in turn?

What are they reciting? Great songs about epic journeys? Long lists of their loves? Improvised prayers? New truths that became clear to them only as they threw themselves into the water? Can they hear one another? Are they speaking to one another? Replying to one another? Are they singing a sailor's song in unison? But not one of the faces seems set on revealing its mystery. Try as she may to invent a story for each of them, their features remain entirely undecipherable.

To get to know them better, she could go down to her desk and consult each one's file. Using their identification card, she could start to sketch out their paths, imagine what drove one or the other toward the shore, these men with their Breton names, their Romanian names; it isn't the same things—the small towns they're from, whether or not they've studied, their age—which cause them to stay in the trade or return to land, swearing not to speak of their knotted stomachs during the first crossings. She could flip through the medical records, the secret documents about the mistakes they've made. Then match the numbers up with each man's naked body. She could toss out first names, throw them just like that from the top of the railing and see who responds. She could shout what's weighing on her heart, too: her long-extinguished loves and this small, recent capitulation, this slowness she has felt for several days.

It's the first time she is alone onboard. This realization electrifies her, and with it comes a clear vision of new possibilities. Rapidly, she calculates how long it will take them to make their way back to the lifeboat, then row through the waves to the ladder that she'll lower to them. So, she moves back from the guardrail, steals away from their sight, and disappears into the forecastle that overlooks the shipping containers. Once on the upper story, a row of doors stretches before her, those of the officers' cabins. She opens one of them, choosing to believe it's at random, sits down, an intruder, on the bunk, and looks around. Rumpled sheets and the smell of a man, papers on the desk, a computer. All she would have to do is power it on to learn everything about the one who lives here. She recognizes her chief mate's suitcase. Would her opinion of the sailor she thinks she knows best change if she uncovered these small objects' secrets? Would she finally know what he's seeking, this man, when they look out to sea together? In one of his pockets, she finds a stone. She, too, picks them up sometimes, like a bit of land you want to take with you. She finds a metro ticket, incongruous here, almost unsettling. A cell phone that she unlocks with a flick of her finger: a photo of a child set as the background, a pretty blond boy with wide open eyes. She didn't want to see this. She turns it off, fingers burned by this reality delivered by an electronic device, incompatible with her, with here. She puts each object back in its place. All she would have to do is make the rounds of the cabins and open the toiletry kits to learn everything about the men: their most hidden fears, their illnesses, their scents, their soaps, their razors, their anti-anxiety drugs, their condoms, their toothbrushes, their creams, their combs, their superstitions, their magical balms, their neuroses, their disorders.

She remembers other incursions into privacy, on land at times, in the home of a man she had met and then followed to his home, when, left alone in the apartment the time it took to run an errand, in the silence that wasn't hers, she would lie languidly on the couch, reach for a sweater left there, smell it, put it on. She would skim a newspaper or a half-read book, would deduce where the man had stopped in his train of thought. She would hear on the landing a door opened then slammed, the neighbors' voices, the sounds of this particular building. She would have the feeling, then, of knowing him better than when he'd told the slightly falsified, slightly awkward stories about his life. Better than when, with self-assurance, he unfurled the respectable CV.

In this officer's cabin, she finds it reassuring that the sailors' absence is filled with so many small things. A pair of socks near the chair says everything about the hurry, the sudden and unexpected departure, like in those ruins where you find objects left in the lurch, ready to be used, just an over-turned vase here and there to recall the catastrophe.

She, too, would like to leave a token of her passage, of her sudden friendship with this group of men, a sort of gesture toward them that she won't dare make once they're onboard again, an errant wink. She would like to briefly inhabit this space, knows she has only a few minutes at most, and so without thinking, she takes off her clothes and gets in the shower. She lathers up with his soap, a supermarket-brand shower gel that faintly hints of sugar or vanilla. She moves her hands over her body as she usually does after her shift, to cleanse herself of the tensions, the technical words spit out into a walkie-talkie in English, and to revive herself a little after the hours of motionless horizon. She puts her clothes back on over her damp skin; it seems as though it's she who controls time, and that by slowing each gesture she can make this moment of solitude last forever.

Alone, of course, it would be difficult to sail, to split herself between the bridge and the engine room, between the head and the guts. She imagines how she could do it, going from position to position, never sleeping.

She would manipulate the controls and ensure the freighter started up again. Dangerously, she would restart the propellers, creating an enormous wave for the swimmers, the distance now impossible to bridge. It would only take one impulse, a sequence of movements within her reach. She would only have to switch off a tiny piece of her conscience. Then, alone on her freighter, she would sail, avoiding land and other boats as best she could, and one day, she'd end up somewhere and would never know how to explain how her men had disappeared. Or on an early morning, just as the fog lifted, the ship would be found thrown up at great speed against a barrier of rocks. People would tell children tales of her disheveled silhouette, her ghostly thinness. She'd like to die this way, in a great uproar, at the mercy of the waves after years of wandering, once the earth had definitively decided it didn't want any part of her.

She knows that some shipwrecks are found without anyone being able to say what happened—neither black box nor distress flare: life abruptly abandoned. And there are those still-feared pirates against whom hatches must be bolted on approaching the coast, those pirate speedboats that pounce in some zones as soon as a freighter slows down. She imagines the blood that curdles at the very moment one understands what is happening. She often thinks about the kind of confrontation that would be— two human enemies in the middle of the ocean, and the certainty of a death without witnesses.

She quits the cabin and walks down the stairs until she's as close as she can be to the water. She could dive from the prow into the ocean, too, and leave the freighter empty of all human presence, with no one to help them back onboard—she and the men—and see what happens when she's no longer in command. Does a shipwreck give rise to new forms of solidarity? In drowning, does flesh become fish? Does skin really grow scales?

# VI

Now, in their minds, it's like a long slow-motion segment in a movie or a nightmare, which ends with a startled jerk. Once again, it's a lightning bolt for the heart, as though they had to go through everything this morning as a cocktail concocted especially for them by the abyss.

When no one is there to hear them anymore, the sound of their voices is a coarse cry, a yelp as shrill as a shameful secret.

Each of them, thinking himself alone, bellows at the apparition.

It's a face. Then another face, finally, as worried as their own, exhausted, red. Each face coming up from the water belongs to a body that is using all its muscles, all its human capacities. Each face sharpens its gaze at the same moment and is relieved to see the familiar lifeboat and buoys, the bathing ladder. Each measures the meters still to be swum and the crosscurrents. And each recognizes the others and smiles at these waves, a little high now, that managed to make them believe that everyone had vanished. So they swim their confident crawl again. A few meters from the lifeboat, they laugh as they did before—virile laughter— and relax, unclenching their muscles.

All at once, they float more easily in the water, breathe maybe a little more fully, reclaim the use of their lungs. And so they reconnect with an immediate future, they who, as they dove, had encountered only their own limits and death laid bare with its white reflections.

They forget their fears and feel full of a pride they've quickly regained, the pride of having been free of every-thing for a moment, audacious, strong, athletic, happy, lucky, chosen, resilient, unique, and alive. They call one another by their first names now, shout out to and con-gratulate each other. They feel affection for this one's reddened skin, that suntan, that strand of tousled blond hair coming out of the water. They rediscover the bridge of one's nose, another's slightly gappy teeth, a wrinkle, a particular laugh. They marvel over a perfect, round ear they'd never noticed before, would like to run their fingers through the wet hair of a sailor whose name they don't even know, and to embrace each other—to say, today, that they love each other with a true love, with a crazy love, and who cares about the lovers left at port? Immersed in joy, they would kiss each other fully on the mouth if only they were close enough to do so; they would look each other in the eyes and run their hands along each other's bodies. After all, they tell themselves, it's these men—the crew, these twenty, their comrades—these men and none other who are their brothers and their mirror, these men who, for forty-five minutes now, have known them more intimately than anyone—this is the number of human beings that they need to survive. The only love is this one in the magic moment, and if in a few hours nothing is left of it, they will have fully lived the euphoria of knowing one another.

In the last few minutes, they've held out their hands to one another. Those who have already hoisted themselves into the small boat catch the others' fingers and pull them aboard. They recognize the comforting contact of these standard motions. The tiny lifeboat serves its function well and saves them from everything. They come together and regroup. Some are first to get into the orange lifeboat, and absolutely no one wants to be the last, the one who struggles, who is slowed by a cramp, the one whose arms or heart play tricks on him.

They're out of breath, and not one of them speaks. They don't know how to begin to formulate a first word without plunging into banalities—worse, they think, than falling back into the deep water. After the shouting and the primitive songs, after the fabulous silence, they no longer know in what language they should start up the engine of little nothings:

"You OK?"

"Yeah, OK."

"Glad to see you."

They look at their feet, securely planted in the bottom of the lifeboat, at the salt marks on their almost dry skin; they look, as though they can't quite believe it, at their men's feet upon the plastic. They know they're pale and trembling. Despite their smiles, the attempted onomatopoeias on their lips, they find that they're pitiful. They didn't believe themselves capable of such terror, when nothing around them should have been cause for panic, there's hardly a breeze to ruffle the water, a little flirtation on the part of the landscape.

They watch one another. Once they've piled into the lifeboat, freezing, not one of them seems more agile in his movements, freer in his body now out of the water. Even that one who has a higher standing in the hierarchies of the ship and work: he has the slightly hollow chest of a skinny child—the depression at the level of his thorax seems to accuse him of defeat.

They are naked and exhausted to a perfectly equal degree.

They know that something has escaped them. For almost an hour, they lost the thread of everything. A few swells played a trick on them. Between the ocean and them, something has happened of which they will never speak, or they'd need to have drunk a lot, or they'd need to have pulled many all-nighters.

When there are no more hands to grab in the water or bodies to hoist toward them, the question arises for the first time: is everyone here? And how to be sure, if no one kept an eye on anyone else? For the first time, they wonder why no one stayed aboard the craft to watch over the others, so that he could tell the story, without calling up ghosts, of what just happened. Each would give everything he has to know, precisely, how far he swam and what the exact height of the waves was. How fast was the wind blowing? How many breaststrokes? Could someone say the precise length of the crawl strokes and breaths held, please? They would give everything to know that someone would have thrown them the lifebelt, that the motor would have sprung toward them should they falter, that someone would have noticed a breathlessness, a shoulder slipping imperceptibly beneath the surface. They go over the security measures backwards in their minds.

They imagine that the captain stayed put, that she was ready to intervene all along; but, as soon as they were in the water, they understood that there was already a world between them and her. They no longer belong to the same element. Their lives weigh slightly less than hers.

*Is everyone here?* their eyes cry out, sweeping over the bodies in all directions and getting lost in all the interlacing hands, the backs that bend toward the water to bring the last men on board. Before counting again, they take in the ocean on all sides, hold their arms out to all the shadows, flinch at the sight of each trail of sea spray.

"The lifeboat is full, isn't it?"

It seems that the bodies are as tightly packed as when they threw themselves into the water. There's no gap to signal an absence, nor any face that surfaces like an alarm in their memory because it hasn't been glimpsed in a long time.

They begin to calm down and the waves carve out their hollows again. They cut a striking image, reminiscent of another painted raft, these naked men sitting motionless on the orange-colored plastic.

And now someone has to decide to move. Someone has to maneuver, to send toward the freighter the signal of their return.

# VII

"1, 2, 3, 4, 5, 6, 7, 8, 9, 10, 11, 12, 13, 14, 15, 16, 17, 18, 19, 20 . . . 21."

No one says anything. After a few seconds, they count again, finally break the silence, bringing each other this comfort.

"We should be twenty," one says. "Count with me again?"

"17, 18, 19, 20, 21. Wait, start again," says another.

"I've started over twice, you count."

"OK: 2, 4, 6, 8, 10, 12, 14, 16, 18, 20 . . . 21. We must have counted wrong to begin with. But I remember twenty even, an even number."

"If I'd known! I don't like odd numbers."

"Oh, stop, we already have enough superstitions, let's not add any."

"Sure, but what if we'd forgotten how to count while we were in the water, that'd be a real problem for navigating."

"No big deal, there are always the machines, impossible to get lost."

"Too bad, it would've been a holiday."

"That wasn't enough vacation for you, our little swim?"

"I mean, not being accountable to anyone."

"But there's always the captain. The captainesse."

They laugh.

"Always the one to know where we're going."

They laugh.

"To keep us in line."

They laugh.

"At her feet."

They laugh.

"Worse than at home."

"So, everything OK? We can start up the motor, go back to the freighter?"

"Since we keep telling you everyone is here."

"Twenty-one. Twenty-one, it's strange, though."

"No, you must have forgotten to count yourself at the beginning."

"Not my style," says the other.

They laugh.

"Not at all like me to mess up numbers. Letters, OK, yes, it happens sometimes, I'll have doubts about spelling, one *l* or two *l*s, one *t* or two *t*s, things like that. But not numbers, not numbers. That's the reason I do this work to begin with, because numbers come easily for me, they make sense to me, I trust numbers."

"So, what sort of work would you have done if you hadn't liked numbers, Mister Poet?"

They laugh.

"Yeah, that suits you: poet."

"I don't have the imagination for it."

"I beg to differ: you imagine what, that numbers change when we go swimming?"

"Well at least we didn't lose anybody."

"Of course not, there was no risk of that."

"There's always a risk, we're nothing out here."

"We're nothing in general."

"Hey, philosopher, were you a little bit scared?"

"That's not why I'm saying it."

"In my day, sailors weren't so afraid."

"They hadn't seen *Jaws*."

"Yeah, but they'd read *Moby Dick*."

"Very funny."

"You there, why aren't you saying anything—you're totally white."

"Not everyone appreciates your jokes."

"Oh, please, are we men or aren't we?"

"Until we're back on board, we're hardly worth more than plankton."

They laugh.

But they're all thinking about that number, twenty-one, thinking about the strangeness of the sound of that number. It's true, there are lots of new ones this time, very young ones, you can lose track, they all look alike, these little muscly guys who thought they were going to discover America or conquer the world. You stop remembering who you traveled with from one time to the next. It's not your fault if the faces change after a port of call, if there are a few of them to whom you've hardly spoken.

A few years ago, contracts were longer. You knew your crewmates, then. Now the deck of cards is reshuffled every time, as though affinities and attachments had to be avoided at all costs. As though all one should think about now is moving forward the machine, alongside young foreigners who will ask for nothing.

—

"Do you see her?" one sailor asks.

"Has she got lost, or what?"

"No, it's that she's lost without us."

They laugh.

"I would've liked to see her swim."

"You mean naked?"

"No, not at all, I mean see her swim, that's all."

They don't laugh, think suddenly of the depth, of the kilometers below.

"She's more cautious than we are."

"You mean less stupid?"

"No, I mean more cautious."

"So, newcomers, are you all OK, did you have a nice little baptism?" But no one responds. It's true, thinks the one who's attempted contact, most of the newcomers don't speak French.

"*Good bath,*" he tries in English, "*big big swimming pool . . .*"

They don't laugh.

"Let it go, have you seen how pale they are, they're always sick, they look like ghosts."

"*Ghosts?*" takes up another, in English.

They don't laugh.

"So where is she?"

"She *is* going to come help us, throw us another ladder, isn't she?"

"Stop freaking out, your sweetheart hasn't abandoned us."

"Don't talk about her that way."

"Wait, guys, are you sure we'll be able to lift up the lifeboat? How many meters is it?"

"Of course, we tie up here and here and then we hoist it from the top."

"But who's going to hoist it?"

"Yeah, well I thought lifeboats were made so that once at sea they stayed there. You're not supposed to come back on board if the freighter's on fire or if it's sinking."

"Oh, yeah? And what if no one's there to help us, do we just hope to find a deserted island?"

"You think you're Robinson Crusoe?"

They laugh.

"You'd do better to shut up and keep your strength for your arms, because now we'll have to climb back up the ladder, it's no time to be weak. She'll be there for us, and then we'll pick up the work where we left off."

"Meanwhile, I don't see her."

"Maybe she jumped overboard."

"Maybe she forgot we exist."

"What if something happened to her?"

"Like what?"

"I don't know, a fainting spell, some girl thing."

"Do you always have to be an idiot?"

"Oh, come on, it's to lighten the mood. No, but seriously, if she injured herself alone on board, we're all responsible."

"How could she have injured herself, she's not working the engines, last I checked."

"Do you want me to list the thousand ways you can injure yourself on a ship?"

"Sure, it would pass the time."

"Give it a rest! Help me to steer."

"Slow down, we're too close to the hull, this is no time to clown around."

"I'm not clowning around, I'm trying to take the waves on the diagonal. We're not trying to send everyone overboard right now."

"A few more meters. Chin up, guys."

"You were right, they're pale: seriously spooked."

# VIII

"So?" she asks, "Everyone back on board?"

"There are twenty-one of us," one sailor says.

"You mean twenty?"

He doesn't say anything.

"Sirs," she says, "thank you in advance for your speed. I'll be happy to see you back in your regulatory uniforms as quickly as possible and ready to pick up your work. It goes without saying that what just happened, this little hiatus, was not marked in our log and that it had best not become a habit or distract us to the extent that we forget our assigned schedule. This is why I ask that you consider it a unique occasion; let us take it as a joyful moment, a party that we organized on board for the pleasure of sharing a powerful moment together. Tell yourselves that it's a gift I wanted to give you in recognition of your work, of your aptness at your task, a reward for your seriousness. It goes without saying that this does not imply, onboard, more relaxed relationships nor any change whatsoever in each person's mission. Obviously, I would like all of this to remain between us: you know how quickly rumors fly and get twisted. I would not want anyone to be able to say that with me everything is permitted, you understand, that I take the crew's lives as something to be played with lightly. You know that isn't the case, you know that I trust you, and I thank you for having followed the safety regulations. I hope no one was injured, I hope . . . I hope, above all, that you had a nice time."

She scans the twenty or so bodies, registers their shame at being naked in front of her, their regret over their decision to be nude so strong it's written on their faces. She knows she could prolong their torture indefinitely by continuing to speak, but she doesn't: it's annoyance that prevails at the sight of the mottled skin, the blue lips and fugitive glances.

She climbs back up to the bridge, waits until each man is back at his station before having the engines restarted. Those who need to rest, rest. The others return to the numbers, the screens. To the kitchens and hallways. To the noise of the engine, the heat that makes them forget that all around them is nothing but water.

And not another word is exchanged anywhere on the ship. They all concentrate as though they were discovering the rules and motions of navigation for the first time, as though they had forgotten the simplest actions, which are now suddenly coming back to them. Old friends rediscovered with joy and self-evidence. The radar, reactivated, confirms that the freighter has moved scarcely a few meters.

She will remember the spot. She bends over to note on the map this unmysterious position in the Atlantic, where it wouldn't have taken much for another ship to cross their route and find itself surprised at their immobility. She pushes down hard on the pencil, so hard she pierces the page, leaving a hole in the paper on the spot where they dove, a possible opening to keep in her memory.

Silently, her chief mate circles around her, ventures a step closer, awkwardly clears his throat. And the annoyance comes over her again:

"What is it? You want to tell me something?"

"No, nothing," he coughs. "But it's funny that you said

twenty earlier, because I also thought we were twenty, and then when I recounted several times, I kept getting twenty-one. I don't know where the error is."

"I don't know, either," she cuts in. "The most important thing is that we didn't lose anyone."

Now she would like everyone to leave her alone again: her solitude didn't last long enough at all. Since she passed through the cabins, she has felt the need to take stock of the group she herself composed, so that she can see the picture of the human strengths and sorrows more clearly. She picks up the pile of folders on her desk and spreads them out in front of her.

There are too many. She blames herself for her negligence. She is usually much more rigorous. She normally doesn't forget, as she did here, to re-file the documents belonging to those who did not, ultimately, come aboard. She usually knows at any moment where each man is; she controls the balance of personalities distributed on the ship, just as she knows the weight of each container and even had them placed in specific spots to distribute the load without any margin of error. There are stories of ships that, due to some mathematical error, find themselves broken in two mid-voyage.

—

Has someone come in and added papers on her desk, to muddle her count? She who usually never locks anything turns the key in the lock behind her. Let no one come and create chaos on her ship, because it's all she knows and the only thing she believes in.

## IX

At mealtimes, they all show up, punctual and serious, whether energetic or weary. They take stock of the latest details about their route; more rarely, they let themselves tell stories about their earthbound lives.

She is in her seat, the first to be served, according to a hierarchy that she would just as soon give up. Today, everything is in order. The talkative talk as though they would like to single-handedly fill in every silence, sew together the bits of time between yesterday and now, close up the smallest breach that might remind them that something happened this morning and that their bodies still bear its trace. The silent listen and eat and do not reply. They wish, perhaps, to relive the plunge and the swim in their thoughts.

Today, she belongs to those who do not speak. She observes their faces. She knows the officers well. Knows that it isn't among them that the discrepancy took hold. And so she gets up and goes over to the side where the other sailors are, those who work on the deck and spend eight hours a day in the engine room. They don't have the same looks as the officers, they speak in interjections to ask for a piece of bread or to toss out a joke. When she enters their refectory, everyone hushes and looks at her, though it's routine enough, this round she makes to ensure that all is well, to lessen as best she can the boundary between their two worlds, between those below and those above, those who sweat in obscurity and those who see the light.

"Hello, men, pardon my interrupting your meal. Is everything OK?"

A mechanical question to which she doesn't really expect an answer. She takes advantage of their silence to scrutinize their faces, immediately spots a newcomer she doesn't recognize, a blond boy, sitting slightly apart from the others. *The one who observes the scene from the edge of the painting* is the thought that crosses her mind, as though

73

this were a time to take an interest in contemplation and composition.

She promises herself that she'll check who he is, where he comes from, and what post he's assigned. She tries to remember his movements in the water, but she gets the particularities of each of these bodies confused. She attempts a smile, leaves the refectory. Is not surprised to hear a few words in an unknown language once she turns her back—and laughter.

"I've checked all the files, all is well," she says, returning to her seat next to her chief mate. "Twenty-one from the start, I have all the ID cards, there can't have been any error."

Why is she lying? She herself has no idea. Partly as a game and partly as a challenge, or in order to put reality back on its straight path by her words alone and thus to extinguish any worries.

They're not running behind. They'll just have to push the engines a little harder to make the port of arrival on time and, as always, moor the freighter at the dock for a few days, enough time to unload and reload the merchandise, an exchange of globalized gadgets for a few local fruits, calculations of mass and weight, manipulation of crates, and that noise of metal clanging on metal that will last all night if necessary.

She must settle the formalities that she knows by heart, the port entry forms that must be submitted once they've arrived at destination, the supporting certificates. The confidential documents about the degree of hazardousness of the merchandise she's transporting, which she will disclose to no one among the crew. She sends in a series of notes the mechanical data and the economic data, the flow, the fees and merchant contracts. She knows she's participating in an absurd, ever-repeated ballet, the choreography of international exchange, of the money that rolls in when arms at the port lift and put in motion, when men in the engine room scorch their faces in a miasma of diesel fumes eight hours a day.

She remembers how reassuring it is for her to get back to work: she likes the numbers, the decisions to be made, the papers to sign. She likes having the impression that if the ship is moving forward, it's in part because of her. And then she stops. Takes out the stack of files again, for which each sailor has provided identity papers and medical certificates, administrative information, work history.

—

So? Who are you, extra sailor? Is it you, blond boy at the edge of the frame? But though she searches through every drawer, in this office where she's once again shut herself away, she finds no document that might correspond to that boy. If he were a stowaway, why would he slip in among the crew, and why suddenly show himself in the middle of a voyage, barely a week before arrival, when it would have been simpler to wait another few days in his accomplice's cabin? And why this journey, leaving Europe behind, with no stop at El Dorado along the way?

All their documents laid out next to one another, all those names and faces, recreate on the table the same magical chaos as earlier in the water, the same haphazard union with its unknown consequences. She's now certain that there was, in that swim, an extreme coherence that she'll seek for a long time to reclaim. A unanimous, electric joy that hasn't stopped coursing through her.

She would be living in a perfect moment in which each element in her life took on a reassuring logic, if it weren't for that wobbly odd number, a hurdle that slows her in her exasperating habit of taking in the world from a soaring height.

—

What is it that came on board along with her sailors? This number that's too large, this doubt where there should never be doubt, since numbers are made for us to rely on. This great weariness. Or this blond sailor, whose file she has in all likelihood simply lost, something she is taking as an error when it may just be a result of absent-mindedness.

She could call the port, ask for a little more information about the last sailors to board, more about the young man, barely an adult, certainly from Eastern Europe, with small eyes so transparent that she should have noticed him before—and she'd know, in black and white, his reason for being there, on her ship, which is slowly starting up again midway across the Atlantic.

She prefers to stash the files at the back of a drawer, which she closes with a quick, brusque movement, then locks. A new habit.

After an hour of reports and signatures, she lets her hands fall onto the desk: they're a map lying before her eyes, with their network of veins and pleats. A territory she's surveyed for thirty-eight years without knowing it, her fingernails sharp as cliffs. Lifting one phalanx after another, she begins to look through her skin, to enter her flesh.

She sees the table through her fingers, a solid, dependable geological layer. She digs farther, wants to sound the depth of things, even to the carpet under the table, trodden by so many men's shoes and cleaned once a week, according to protocol. Then she sees the metal that separates the structure's various floors, isolating, as best it can, the officers from the other sailors, the offices from the bunks. She passes through them to the empty cabins just below her, and the one where a man sleeps because he has worked all night. Her eyes pierce the sleeping man, and by way of his unmade bed, by way of his clothes scattered on the floor, she finds the metal under the thinner, shabbier, more scuffed carpet. She digs down to the engine itself, its pipes and pistons, its vapors and liquids. She pauses a moment at the screens and knobs, at a few men bustling in their workman's blue. Passing through them, she notices how tired their legs are; still, she doesn't stop at them but burrows deeper, to the depths of the ship.

Then the last floor takes on the golden-brown color of scales, and just below: a vast, living heart, an enormous piece of red flesh that contracts with a deaf pulsing and throbs out a beating amplified by the hull. She sees the blood that spurts from the heart and floods the whole freighter from below, a network of blue and red arteries, veins and venules interwoven so the ship can float.

So this is what the rumbling was. This is what, for days, has been purring beneath her feet, beneath her bed. It's a heart beating under her own. She hears it so clearly now that it moves her a little. As the freighter picks up speed, it beats faster and faster. It's criss-crossed with joy and fury—any more and it would howl. It rages. It won't stop breathing.

She listens to this body. She who has never listened to her own.

It's euphoric, set free now on the sea, in the letting go, the long glide. Whereas at port, like her, it chomps at the bit, almost whines at having to idle, to remain unmoving in place, manipulated, a beast of burden, tied firmly to the dock, wedged tightly between the gantry cranes. Nice, domesticated horse.

It's wild, essentially. It only returns to the outskirts of cities when forced to do so, like those sailors who yield to land because someone is waiting for them there, so that their bodies can be buried at the foot of a tree, a sign of earth's victory over water.

—

She wants to place her hands on the animal's haunches, to feel their warmth, let herself be carried away by the disruption this would stir up, to press her fingers, like a lover's, against the vibrating skin. Palms open, she gives in to this gliding on the sea, to this burning in the pit of her stomach.

# X

Those transparent eyes. They're the first thing she catches sight of when she opens her office door to return to the bridge. Those transparent eyes that transfix hers before disappearing around a bend in a corridor. She doesn't like the cold sensation of those eyes, their fog-white color.

"Excuse me?" She raises her voice a little, and the boy reappears: "Can you remind me which station you work? I believe this is the first trip we've taken together. Have you been with the company long?"

Incredibly, he replies by shrugging his shoulders, then points to his mouth, split into a smile.

"You're . . . I'm sorry, I didn't know, you're mute?"

He shrugs his shoulders again, does a very slow

about-turn, and resumes his journey down the corridor, toward the stairs that lead to the engine room.

She feels ridiculous as she rarely does at the words she's just stammered; usually, she consigns moments like these to a black notebook that she later destroys, part of a yearly ritual summoning all the magic forces of amnesia.

She would like to call her chief mate. To have him at her side immediately, witness to this encounter. So he could give her an explanation. She would like to cry his name and have him come running from the other side of the ship. But there's no one around her office at this hour. Everyone is at his station.

She doesn't know whether to follow him to his cabin —this pale boy—playing on her authority and stalking him until he speaks, or to pull herself up, dignity intact, and not take as an affront what was likely a misunderstanding, linguistic and cultural. It's not the first time, old girl, that something won't translate, that you can't find the right words to speak to them, the youngest, the inexplicable sailors, those who come aboard driven by a romantic spirit or simply in order to survive, without knowing the first thing about sailing. The codes, old girl, you know very well that when someone doesn't know the codes of your world—and, presumably, doesn't want to know them—you collapse in on yourself and on your absurdities.

She straightens her back in the stifling corridor and tries to climb calmly to the bridge.

"Captain, look. What is it?"

Barely through the door, and she's called on, ever expected to be the solution to everything. It takes her a few seconds to figure out what the helmsman is talking about: the first surprise is that he's come out of his silence at all. She notes his careful diction, his nasal voice.

"What do you mean, what is it? You've never seen mist?"

She cuts him off. She no longer wants—that's it—to let herself be affected by anyone's fear, by a flicker of doubt in anyone's eyes; she wants the numbers and seascapes to go back to the way they were.

"I've seen mist," he continues. "But not here, not so suddenly . . . Shouldn't we make a detour?"

"What does the forecast say?"

"The forecast says there's nothing. Clear skies in the entire zone."

"The forecast isn't infallible. Keep going. Straight ahead."

She can feel the man stiffen, senses that she's just lost all her points in the great game of trust. But for now she doesn't know why she should entertain everyone's fears and superstitions. White masses, cold vapors—she's certainly crossed them on other trips.

She hadn't seen it. For an hour or two, between the office and the passageway, she forgot to look outside. And so she lost touch with the most essential thing: the ocean, its state, its color, its surface. Her eyes finally focus outside of herself, and, through the large windows, she sees that the horizon has in fact been erased, swallowed by a white sky.

As though she has to register things through her skin—always her skin—to understand what is happening to her, she pulls open the metal door and goes outside. She wants to feel the consistency of this fog, to know its temperature. There—this will be her swimming.

Immediately, the dampness of this condensed storm seizes her. It's as though they've been rolled up into a cloud, a cloud that she robotically, instinctively tries to hold between her splayed fingers. White cotton candy that's almost sweet by sheer dint of density: because no one can see her, she sticks out her tongue to taste it. One has to fall back on a few childhood instincts when it feels like nothing funny will happen anytime soon.

The farther she moves away from the door, the harder it is to breathe. She feels like she's swallowing buckets of water every time she inhales, but she's lived enough years with the taste of salt on her skin to not panic at this impromptu encounter between air, sky, and ocean.

She takes a few more steps. It would take much more for her to lose her bearings on this ship whose proportions are so like all the others that she could easily cross it from end to end, with her eyes closed, without running any risk.

But in the whiteness, the vertigo is more intense, so she stretches her hands out in front of her and slows her step. All she'd need, on top of everything else, is for a swell to come and play at throwing her to the ground. But that prank isn't in the cards today: the waves are even surprisingly calm in this spot.

—

A few voices begin to make themselves heard around her: several men have also come up onto the deck. More cautious than she is, they venture in twos and threes, holding each other's shoulders. They grasp at the air that surrounds them, palpate the mist as though it were their first snow, then come back to their bodies. *What do they still need to wash themselves of?* is the odd question that arises in her as she makes out their forms, a few steps away.

The others have stayed behind the windows; already, their beautiful collective spirit is fissured by wariness. They are sailors whose eyes have just been blotted out by strange weather, and they haven't yet had the time to develop tools other than their vigilance and their complaints. On the bridge, the helmsman has just experienced his sudden uselessness and now falls back on the radar—far less likely to be intimidated than he is. A sailor coming back from his break believes he's still asleep in his bunk. With his eyelids so heavy, how can he really tell the difference? Those sailing for the first time feel their throats tighten a little more than the others; but, after all, that's been the case from the outset of their journey, every time something deviated from the image they'd made of the job or of its landscapes. The most hardened sailors have placed this mist in the category of basic annoyances, like everything else that requires them to be more focused on their task when what they've developed is a taste for drifting.

*It looks cut from the worn sheet of a ghost,* is the other strange thought that crosses her mind and, immediately, she remembers certain dreams she's had that leave her with a racing heart. Always, there is an invisible presence in a room that ruffles the curtains or moves the furniture slightly, a shadow that awaits her on a window ledge, a malicious breeze that seeks to frighten her. Used to this dream, she tries, when it recurs, to listen to the invisible force, awaiting a revelation, as they say some dreams bring them; but there's nothing, no clue to reveal who is causing a book to fall, a chair to move. Sometimes it seems to her that it's a hand, a hand that fails, night after night, to place itself on her back.

Now, she's in the same state of waiting: perhaps all it would take is to know how to read the mist in order for a sign or explanation to appear. Or she might have to reach out a hand, to pull back once and for all this recurrent curtain to know what it conceals. But everything has decided to be blind and mute, and her eyes sting from trying to pierce the milky white.

All she knows is that the pulsing is still there, under her feet—the red beating under the white mass. A force that imperceptibly heats and softens metal.

Hold on, animal. It's only a slight slippage in the day. If you trust me, we'll soon pick up the calm version of this story again.

Saying this, she remembers that she's still the one steering the ship. She doesn't know how long she's stayed here, wrapped in fog, without taking a step or making a single movement. Around her, the voices have long been silent, each man has returned to his station. But she knows that wonders are short-lived, that you become used even to the breathtaking sights on each journey.

She turns around and feels her way toward the door. Outside, the danger suddenly seems too great that something could decide to brush against her, to seize her by the collar and make her fall into an ocean of absurdities. Back inside the ship, she crosses the border again, the one that separates the mist from normalcy by cutting out a square of breathable air at the bridge.

—

The helmsman is still in the same position, absorbed by the concentric circles on his screen. So maybe she hasn't been gone so long.

"What does the radar say?"

"Nothing. Look. It says that we're alone in the middle of this white desert."

# XI

"Captain, captain, don't you see anything coming?"

She doesn't flinch when the chief mate speaks just behind her. Without having heard him, she sensed that he was coming, knew that he would be there soon to light her way through the thick wool of her thoughts.

"Only that the ocean is getting whiter, and the sky . . . the sky is, too."

"Such an odd blanket."

"You noticed? We can't even see our own containers anymore."

"Yes. The crew is worried. It's unusual for there to be mist here."

—

She turns to him. She knows him well enough to know with what finesse he's introduced this idea of worry. He must have weighed this word and all the other words, must be coming to speak with her on behalf of a crew that's been made vulnerable all of a sudden. Without appearing to insist, his face now seems simply to be awaiting an answer. She could take and squeeze his hand to thank him for this tact.

With a tilt of her head, she invites him to go toward the map; she's surprised by the hole she herself punched a few hours earlier.

"I know everyone is worried. I've gone over and over the situation in my head, the position doesn't correspond to any land. To any obstacle. It must have to do with an abrupt variation in temperature. I think we'll have to get used to these changes in the climate. We'll have to stay on the alert."

Before he can reply, she adds, as though a trivial thought had just flitted through her mind:

"Do we have a deaf-mute sailor among the crew? Among the Romanians, the Polish, the newcomers? The ones who work the engine. A blond boy, with these eyes. Does that ring a bell?"

She's spoken a little too quickly, once again in that too-shrill voice that doesn't suit her and makes her regret each word she speaks.

"I don't think so," he replies, "I had individual interviews with them before we boarded. Why? Is there a problem?"

"No problem. I was just wondering, that's all."

"There's another thing, captain."

She raises her eyes toward him, surprised by a slight change in his voice and by his calling her captain again given the seriousness of the situation—usually it's a little game they play, knowing full well that on land, they call each other by their first names, meet sometimes to talk about their trips at a bar in the city where they both live.

"It seems that we're not able to pick up speed. We're checking everything, we've identified no technical problem for now. And of course there's enough fuel, no leak there."

"Good."

She waits a moment, because something in her chest has pinched, and she doesn't like this feeling.

"Keep looking and keep me informed."

"I'm taking my break," the helmsman announces, although the chief mate already left the bridge several minutes ago.

"You're right to do so. I should, too. I hadn't noticed that our colleagues were already ready to pick up the shift."

She knows that the cabin won't protect her from anything, not even from her own violence. But she goes down, splashes water on her face. She lies on the ground to hear the beating heart of the machine again.

They've lost several knots in a few hours. This bank of mist is pushing them back like a magnet, trying to make them change their course. Oh no, sea, you won't reject us, too, like the most treacherous of shorelines.

"We're pushing the engines as much as we can, but it's no good. It seems as though the ship is deciding on its own speed," the chief mate had said, squinting his eyes and laughing a little.

"You who love a challenge."

She had tried to smile.

What are you doing to us? Animal boat, what are you afraid

of? What are you trying to tell us? What do you want to show us? Is it this mist that's dampening your enthusiasm? Was it when we shut off the engines, a while ago, that you claimed your independence? Animal boat, I hope it's not an illness, not a surrender in the middle of the ocean. Not a heaviness like mine.

Come on, animal, respond. You can see that I'm listening to you. Do you, too, have an idea in the back of your mind? Are you going to dive suddenly like a whale, to carry us into the abyss?

Lying on her cabin's worn carpet, she looks at the sky through the ceiling and at the burning sun behind the mist. It's become very hot in the last few hours of the journey, hotter even than when they decided to swim. With one hand, she unbuttons her shirt and looks for something lighter to wear, unties her hair to hide her shoulders. She breathes in and realizes how thick and damp the air is despite the air conditioning, the ventilation, the thermostats that give everyone the illusion that they're not constantly manhandled by the climate, by the tropical furnaces and the icy winds. Outside, it's no better: the salty water and the smell of diesel that grips the throat. She should do

94

what they did earlier: dive, swim, trace her own path. Fill her nose and mouth with seawater once and for all, cleanse herself of the grease of these machines.

## XII

Within a few hours, they've gone from the abstraction of blueness to the precision of their task, each mobilizing the knowledge acquired throughout his lifetime—the technical names and motions—to try to identify the problem. And while they focus with all their energy on an electrical circuit or the shape of a nut, it's other stories that come into their heads, a wave of tales, the adventures that befell others at sea and that were passed down from generation to generation in order to give each other chills on stormy nights.

They can't shake these tales of the Atlantic and of Atlantis, of the worrisome triangles and ghost ships, while the contradictory results pile up.

"There's nothing abnormal here. It should work."

—

"When I was a student," says a tall, thin guy with a spark of excitement in his voice, "there was this story. A real state secret. Impossible to find out more about what really happened. A freighter that was steering toward the Azores suddenly headed north, toward Newfoundland. Impossible to establish contact with anyone on board. For a week, no one knew if they were dead or alive, if they would stop one day or founder on the reefs. People imagined a hijacking, a hostage-taking, but days passed without any demands, without any news of violence. I don't know if other boats were sent out to meet them; the police and border patrol must have taken action. In short, one day the ship stops and the crew is found, and not one person is able to say how they changed course so abruptly. Something must have happened that had to remain secret, that it was best not to know."

"What are you talking about down there?"

"Nothing, it's just our ghost story specialist again."

"Nothing, nothing. Meanwhile, have any of you figured out where the problem is coming from?"

"There was also this story," offers another, more timid man, now that the door is open to grand tales, embellished just enough to create a bond that lasts as long as it takes to

97

carry out an umpteenth technical diagnostic. "This story of the crew that mutinied against the higher ranks, having decided not to reach the destination port but to stage a fake shipwreck and calmly flee to another continent with part of the cargo."

"Don't count on me for that kind of adventure. Considering what we're carrying."

"And what are we carrying? Do you know?"

"It's not too hard to imagine. T-shirts made in China, furniture kits and liters of Coca-Cola."

"Wheat. Fruit in refrigerated boxes."

"Dangerous substances, maybe—all sorts of radioactive stuff."

"And no one knows the story of our captain's father? He was also part of the company in the eighties."

"Stop, that's a rumor: nothing was ever proven."

"It's a legend, old man, and since when are we not allowed to recount legends on ships?"

"Tell the story, go ahead, I don't know it."

"It's the story of a great captain who'd seen it all, who'd circumnavigated the globe, a captain people cited as an example for the way he could weather a storm. One very calm day, he started a route to South America."

"You're totally embroidering there, but go on, we're listening."

"No, I swear, it was Argentina. Well, the point is, the trip is going normally, the arrival is signaled at La Plata, the harbor pilot is waiting, ready to come meet the ship. And then nothing. One day, two days, three days, no news, no contact, and what's more, no other boat can spot the ship in the zone where it had nevertheless arrived. Everyone is on the alert, preparing divers and a rescue team. And then, after about a week, the signal returns, the ship is right there where it was supposed to be and makes its entry as planned. With just a slight lag. One week lost in the meanderings of time and space."

"And the sailors? What did they say?"

"It's said they didn't notice anything out of the ordinary, and that they were very surprised by the panicked welcome. Above all, they say that the captain didn't open his mouth for several years. No one knows what he saw, but something in him had changed, pretty profoundly."

"Well it doesn't seem very hard to find out. There's someone on board who must know much more about all this than we do."

"So go ahead, ask her."

"Leave her alone."

Sustained by stories and questions, they smile and start working again. They're like those insects that keep their world turning with a rigor that makes them impervious to all mystery. They hunt down the missing bolt, the tiny fissure in one of the tanks; they test, switch from electronic to manual mode, trusting nothing but their own arms activating the levers, setting the pistons to work even in the immense heat of the engines. They consult user manuals, search deep in their memories for specific cases, for the little flaws in the system that someone must once have told them to be wary of.

Four hours go by in concentration and the most profound silence.

They're sweating it because they don't know why the numbers on the dials keep decreasing; they know that at this rate, within a few hours the engines will fall silent again, leaving them with the vertigo of their smallness in the middle of the ocean. With this fog bank as the only horizon. And they don't want that.

Some of them are already annoyed that they've been left to search for the malfunction without any help, no call sent out to other ships with other engineers who could come to their aid with a new perspective and spare parts. These men keep searching without much conviction, awaiting the moment they'll be told not to worry, to relax, let go, give in to being towed, to being rescued. They hope to soon be able to entrust their doubts and fatigue to strangers.

But the freighter hasn't stopped its course. It's not a complete breakdown, just a deceleration, a laziness, an incapacity to master the speed of their journey. They can't yet admit defeat, can't consider themselves abandoned on the water and at the mercy of the currents, forced to activate the distress signal.

Calmly, the boat continues to break through the waves and the schools of fish, still purring its mechanical song, simply possessed of an autonomy that makes humans useless, and makes them understand it.


"Do we have any contact with the outside? Did anyone respond to the report she sent?"

"What report are you talking about?"

"She must have written a report, signaled something, been in contact with the offices, with the port authorities."

"Yes, she must have done that."

"No one knows? No one's asked her? And where is she, in fact? Still locked in her office? I don't like that."

"Calm down, she's working. She's looking for an answer, too."

"You know, before," one man begins quietly, articulating slowly to make sure his French colleagues understand him, "a while ago, when we were swimming, I thought she was going to leave us all alone, that she was going to leave us there. Tiny fish in the wrong fishbowl. And now," he hesitates a little, straightens himself up, knows he risks being met with a general burst of laughter. "Now I'm afraid she'll do something to us. That she'll do something bad to us."

And, against all expectations, no one wants to laugh. No one even answers.

# XIII

He keeps a stone in the pocket of one of his jackets. A gray and white pebble he picked up on the beach on a day of skipping stones. He had wanted to show his son how to bounce them off the water, but he stopped when the boy suddenly became serious, seeing a red freighter motionless on the horizon.

"Do ships that leave always come back?"

"You want to know if I'll always come back from my trips?"

"No, I want to know if there are boats that never come back."

"Long ago, yes, there were boats that disappeared at sea: they weren't as sturdy as they are now, and there wasn't any radio to alert anyone when there was a problem.

Today, boats come back. And they come back faster. I've shown you how fast boats go."

And the stone stayed in his pocket, a token of a worry.

The chief mate places the pebble on the table and composes a message on his phone, one that will be sent out when they're near land again. He deletes it. Starts over. He knows that every word will create fear or anger if it isn't well chosen, if it seems too vague or too detached. If it doesn't come at the right time. He knows that a silence between two messages will awaken jealousy and torment in the depths of his wife's black eyes. That whatever he does, he will cause pain. He writes that today he brushed up against the abyss, that he felt vertigo's caress as he dove into the open sea, as he swam like a child. He knows that he'll never send this message to anyone. He deletes it. He says that, here, the weather is playing tricks on them and that it makes for a bit of adventure—then deletes it. No anxiety. And never the word "adventure."

In the beginning, he'd sent photos of the horizon, had thought that his passion would become shareable, that it would be reassuring to show, day after day, all angles of this vast ship on the water. But whatever he said, it was too egotistical. To marvel at a wave or at the sun was already to betray his love and marriage and this family that already had to function without him more than six months out of the year.

So, as always, he says nothing about the ship or about the sea, nothing of his strenuous rhythm, nothing of the technical conversations at mealtimes, nothing of the night-cap he drinks to summon sleep. He ends up rolling out, mechanically, the words of love, trying not to write the same ones as yesterday. Trying to fill them once again with a unique and powerful sentiment. But he can't. He deletes. He resigns himself to asking about the boy. I love you both.

When he's back on land, he'll try once or twice to talk about the fear that grips him, too, sometimes, of never coming back, of not knowing who he is nor to which life he belongs. He'll try to explain how at sea you have to cling to your wits more firmly than elsewhere, how you have to check your thoughts every day the same way you check the latitude, the longitude, and the engines. He'll talk about how some winds bring joy, madness, improvidence.

But he'll stop before pronouncing the first word, because his wife's gaze will silence him, because open-ing that door would mean days of tears for her, her body wracked by spasms and accentuated thinness. So he'll focus on concrete projects: will spend his time scanning real estate listings and imagining projects, redoing the garden wall, changing the kitchen cabinets, maybe even the car, never pausing to rest, waiting for the next departure.

He'll try to tell his son how happy he is, how much he loves the challenge of making all that metal float on water. How much he loves no longer being tied to any land and not being able to call anyone for days, even if he worries about the boy, even if he doesn't like to imagine not being there if something were to happen to him. He won't tell the boy anything but reassuring stories about work and routine, only the speeches parents serve up in families so the children grow up strong.

He leaves the phone next to the pebble and the metro ticket that reminds him that, once, he tried to leave, to abandon the too-new house for a studio apartment in Paris. That after a few days he turned around again, resumed his role and his responsibilities, hung the curtains, built a second wall, buried this story at the far end of the little garden.

Something else bothers him during this break he allows himself, even though he can sense the agitation everywhere around him, the instructions shouted into walkie-talkies.

On a piece of paper, he writes the number twenty-one and tries to mentally list all of his colleagues. But an image blocks him, keeps him from concentrating. It's that face that surfaced near him when he thought he was lost, left alone at sea and too far away from the life-boat. A smooth and serious face, and—this is what struck him—not out of breath at all. An abnormally calm face mid-swimming.

"Is this your first time sailing with her?"

On the deck, two officers are sharing a cigarette.

"Oh, no, you know I've known her since we were twenty. A nice girl. A hard worker. Wasn't easy for her to make her own name, to not just be her father's daughter. Especially since he came out of nowhere. Not from any family known in the field. A workman's son who decided one day when he saw the sea that he'd steer one of those big ships, too. Worked his way up with no money, hardly enough to pay for a student's room by taking on nights in a bar. A total anomaly. As for her, she always wanted to follow in his footsteps. To never go back. To the life of land-dwellers, as she says.

"Does her father still sail?"

"No. He was declared unfit about ten years ago. No one ever really knew why. A sort of dementia, memory gaps, an absence that became more and more noticeable."

"That story people tell about him, that he disappeared for several days—is it true?"

"There's another version. They say that during the trip, on one of the last days, the boat was struck by a bad wave."

The two men shiver together as if a forbidden phrase, full of sinister magic, had been uttered and now they had to find a way back to a conversation that would exorcise this darkness and reassure them. Together, they saw the wave coming out of nowhere, the wall of water, impossible to predict, that takes a boat by surprise from time to time. They plunged, together, into every sailor's nightmare: the black mass, several meters high, that can single-handedly destroy every point of balance.

"Is that the reason he didn't speak for several weeks? And neither did his crew?"

"I honestly don't know what can explain a thing like that."

After the second cigarette they could go back inside—it's rare for them to exchange even this many words at once—but they both have the slow movements of those who want to prolong a moment of connection, of those who still have worries to share.

"I was asking you whether you knew her well, well enough, because . . . I've heard things. They say she's changed. They say she's a little strange. That a while ago she followed one of the sailors in a corridor, and that she tried to force several cabins' doors."

"Which sailor?"

"One of the newcomers."

And what might have lent itself to an off-color joke a few days ago doesn't make either of the two men laugh.

"Why would she have done that? She could just have called him to her office, if she had a bone to pick with him."

"That's what I'm saying. It's not like her to not follow protocol."

Sitting on her bed now, her knees drawn into her chest, she can feel that doubts are spreading every time two or three men who share the same language cross paths on the ship. She can feel how confidence could flake away if only they scratched a little, if only they found a little rust, a possible entry point, a leak.

If she decided never again to leave her cabin—to let the great ship do its will and lead them wherever it wanted—it wouldn't take long for them to understand that they didn't need her, that together they had the capacities they needed to steer the freighter. But she doesn't feel at all threatened by the idea of such a mutiny. On the contrary, she thinks that it would be joyful, all these men together creating a new order, no longer expecting anything from her and finally focused on mapping out their own path.

She knows that there is something powerful in this group, a humanity that aspires upward, the possibility, perhaps, of inventing something new, or of bringing down one of the small barriers in this world.

She closes her eyes and prepares to let herself be drawn down into the floor again, to lose herself in the hollow of the hull.

But it isn't like her, this retreat in the middle of the day, this abandonment of her station.

She has to walk, to speak, to act: usually, she's three steps ahead, her body totally taut. To stop her, it would take the shock of an image larger than herself, a landscape's composition, a sea creature encountered against all odds.

Last night, it was a certain light. It was no different than if a sharp pain or a fall had stopped her in her tracks, but no: everything was stable, calm. In the last rays of the sun, the sea was hemorrhaging—you could see on its surface a boiling wound, an old memory of a bloody catch, of a hand-to-hand struggle. The water looked scummy, thick and red.

She had stayed for several minutes, until the impression faded, and then she had rubbed her eyes.

It was just before dinner. She thinks about it again now, from her bed, and the dots connect each event to the present moment: how can anyone sail without taking into account the signs the ocean gives us of its moods?

"Something's lodged in your big heart, ship. A harpoon, invisible and powerful. The death sentence for a few of our certainties. You were swimming in your own blood, when all I had on my mind was the routine and the evening's little housekeeping rituals."

## XIV

She's gathered the crew in the wardroom. Not everyone is here; a few have stayed at their stations. When their eyes started to tire, when tensions started breaking their backs and taxing their shoulders, they passed the baton. She thanks them for their work, reassures them that the itinerary hasn't changed, that at most they may be a few hours off-schedule. She reassures, assuring them that she is in contact with the company and with the rescue units, that all is well, that all is well. She recites, without appearing too mechanical, the doublespeak that manages to keep a crew's courage intact. She nails the phrases and procedures so firmly together as she speaks that there's no room for doubt to intrude; she squares her assertions like straight boards you can count on. And while she lowers the well-sealed lid on her speech, she looks for the transparent eyes that crossed her path in the corridor, and doesn't find them.

When everyone else has returned to his station, she stays back with the chief mate. She pulls out a book at random from the small bookshelf. She turns the pages mechanically while she talks to him without looking into his eyes. "Do you know it? The story of a volcano and a loss of control."

Because he doesn't know what else to do, he suddenly moves toward her and takes the novel from her hands. It's the most intimate gesture they've ever shared, but she doesn't flinch, makes no move to back up.

"Do you want me to take over? To communicate with the port? Take care of the administrative things?"

"Why?"

"To practice. I plan to take your place one day, captain a ship myself in the months to come."

A few centimeters from each other, they manage to smile.

He knows the only thing that will save him is to take things into his own hands, to focus on navigating and only navigating, to neutralize, through working, the blurriness he feels in her.

The novel is ever so gently placed back on the shelf, as though it were the thing containing an explosive charge that had to be precipitously defused.

"You have to keep the things you don't know at arms length. To be more stubborn than the ship. You see, sometimes you yourself have to be the great metal body. Hard and mobile, and ready to be moved and blocked. Because that's what it is, the sea, those kilometers under the hull. Because that's what it means to abandon the path of solid earth and roadmaps. We think we'll determine everything when we're at the controls. And we decide hardly anything at all. We don't decide what joins us on board that we won't easily be able to throw overboard. We don't decide on that slab of rock we encounter behind a fog bank."

"I thought there wasn't anything in particular on the radar."

"It's a metaphor."

"Seriously. The guys are worried. They're wondering if you really signaled that we were in distress."

"In distress? What distress? Do you see distress anywhere? We're going to find out why we're decelerating, and we'll arrive at port in the next three days. I don't want to spend this trip explaining in triplicate reports why we're not operating at regulatory speed or why this morning we decided to treat ourselves to a swim."

They don't know it yet, but her full stop and her tone, which is firm once again, are a signal for the mist outside to begin to dissipate a little. It's nothing spectacular, but the vise around their throats loosens imperceptibly.

The closer they get to the tropics, the more the sun falls directly into the sea—and more quickly each night. Soon it'll be nighttime and this day will be a painful memory, consigned to the technicality of the ship's log so it's forgotten more easily.

*I, the undersigned on my own behalf, sea captain, as was my father, first-class captain of maritime navigation, captain of the ship whose heart beats on its own, having as home port a dreary city, and belonging to the shipping company of they who move over the water without second thought, whose headquarters are located in an even bigger city, which makes me feel even more undesirable, declare to have set sail from Saint-Nazaire on an even-numbered day in the twenty-first century, with the West Indies as destination, without knowing that they were shifting, equipped with my orders, the ship being in a good* state of seaworthiness, the regulatory tests and checks carried out before departure having confirmed the proper functioning of the devices and navigational aids, hatches well sealed, water-tight doors secured, cranes tied up at their stations, full crew composed of twenty men and one woman, then twenty-one men and one woman, without the nature of this augmentation being resolved, the woman in question not having given birth and desiring under no circumstances to give birth, loaded with one hundred and fifty thousand tons of various foodstuffs distributed among colored containers, my favorite ones being blue—I find them visually more interesting at dusk on the open sea—the drafts being, at the time of departure, 18.30 meters at the stern and 15.60 meters at the bow.

Left the dock at 22:40 local time, aided by one harbor pilot and assisted by four tugboats. The radar-assisted navigation revealed no malfunction. The navigation took place without any difficulty under clear weather conditions and a visibility of ten miles, at the speed of 12.5 knots. Until a luminous idea crossed the minds of the crew, who were seized by a desire for fresh air, for a little vacation. All of the required preparations for this new situation were made at 9:45 the next morning: professional reflexes on standby, speed reduced to a standstill, engines prepared to maneuver—but human manpower absent, as all were occupied by swimming—regulatory *lights and sound signals working, deactivation of the anti-collision radars.*

*Since that time, report has been made of the ship's becoming totally self-determined and refusing, despite various summons, to respect the speed indications given by the personnel navigating. The breach, considered serious, is inscribed in the disciplinary ledger. The ship nevertheless refused to affix its signature at the end of the document. We are contemplating what actions to take in this matter, even as this insubordination amuses us greatly.*

*As of this writing, it's been decided by me, knowing full well the sanctions to be incurred, to not keep this journal any longer. To not send a report to the destination port. To not speak about the desire I have, in turn, to dive into this fog bank that stretches across the horizon, and to sleep for one hundred years.*

*I affirm that the present report is sincere and true, reserving for myself the privilege of appending or amending it if necessary, and submit it to the registry of the commercial court of Le Havre for all legal intents and purposes.*

—

Stamp, signature, stamp, stamp. Satellite transmission of the daily data: the flimsy things that reassure us.

From behind her porthole, she watches the sun pierce the fog in order to better dive into the water in a lovely orange vertical line, which a last shred of fog spreads with thick strokes. That ochre trail of blood again, but she'd rather see the scar than the wound, would rather that starting tomorrow they could regain the voyage's blue health.

Later on, an incantation, mute and without addressing itself to any particular divinity: rain falls violently on the ship, an evening rain. A tropical rain. A normal rain between two stretches of mist.

For the hundredth time, she checks the weather report on her screen. (And isn't this Weather Report the divinity we summon, in a way, even if we usually dream of being beholden to something far greater than that?) But the forecast doesn't seem to know anything about the expanse of ocean she's crossing. She does have the impression that they're coming closer to the normal humidity level for this place and the season. She tells herself that at least, the way things are going, in a few hours she'll have regained clear visibility.

Six months ago, it was in heavy rain that she'd asked her eyes to be radars (though she was on land) and her legs to not feel so heavy in the puddles. She herself didn't know where to start searching. On a boardwalk usually made to be reassuring—merry-go-round and ice cream vendor in summer, evenly spaced shrubs slightly exotic for the country—everything became hostile with these buckets of water sluicing; a torn poster for a forgotten circus floated in a puddle, and slowing cars betrayed their loss of confidence. There, she had thought, this is what I can't stand here anymore: these moments when we're so profoundly let down by the landscape. But she continued to run, heavily, and to call her father amid the screeching tires.

He had left an hour earlier—she stopped by his place more and more often now, even though he would have hated to think that he might one day need looking after, and that his daughter would have to do anything other than follow her own path and her own adventure. Did he still know that she was there for him and that they were father and daughter?

When she'd seen that the storm wasn't letting up, she was seized by a panic that she'd started to feel about him since he'd stopped speaking. Not being a mother, she could only imagine this was the panic you sign up for year after year when you have a child, a panic that makes you get up at night to check on breathing, that keeps you on the surface of slumber, always an ear cocked, alert for monsters.

Instinctively, she headed for the marina where he went to sit for hours at a time since he'd stopped sailing. As she feared, the port's rocks and water were muddled in the deluge: one step too many and you could fall into the black water, between two yachts deserted for the winter.

Finally, she had spotted his silhouette coming toward her, walking without staggering along the road, as though the liters of rainwater were only a vision come from her own imagination—her eyes had always spilled too much water at the least emotion he'd always told her, since she was a little girl.

She had calmed her steps, had let the icy water drench her.

Here and now—she confirms this as she goes out onto the deck once again, under the illusion that she'll be able to light her cigarette—the water is almost warm: even in her hair and on her neck it manages to be not unpleasant.

—

She'd forgotten that episode of frantic searching in the rain of Toulon. She had erased from her memory that long moment of hesitation, standing stock-still in a puddle, wiping her face with her sleeve as she wondered if she should catch up with her father, thread her arm under his and guide him silently back home. Or simply follow him from afar, letting him believe in their reciprocal independence, and then hand him dry clothes because he'd have already forgotten he was soaking wet.

She'd forgotten that there'd been that final walk by the port and that afterward his health had slowly declined, that he never left the house again. Today, she thought of those months that followed like dry, cold blocks she was constantly bumping into, searching for what they had been, a father and daughter between whom thoughts circulated effortlessly, all they needed was a hint in order to read each other and know what to do about their funny presence in the world.

In the warm rain, she rubs her forearms—come on, old girl—offers herself this little gesture of consolation.

When she closes the door to the bridge, she knows where to find the carefully folded towel for cases like this. She begins by slowly wiping her face. The familiar sensation of the terry cloth towel—to dry the rain on her neck, at the base of her skull—and the smell of that warm, normal rain slowly lets her find her axis again.

What we hold onto.

At the same time, on the other side of the ship, a sailor who is running to get out of the rain trips over a boy lying on the ground. He just manages to grab the guardrail and starts yelling.

But the boy on the ground is very much alive: impassive, he barely blinks, watching the rain fall on his face.

"Whoa! What are you doing? Are you totally nuts? Why are you here, are you hurt, are you OK?"

And the one lying down just shrugs and smiles, breathing in the warm rain that's now entering his nostrils.

"I almost killed myself, you're in the way, you understand when I'm speaking to you? You not stay here, you work like everybody else, you understanding that we be in deep enough shit? And who are you anyway? Do we know each other?" And then in English: *"What is your name?"*

Met with the absence of a response, the sailor angrily clenches his fists and promises himself that next time, he'll get what's coming to him, this boy with a face so smooth that he must not have worked much in his life; next time he'll file a report about this endangering of others by lying in the corridors—when he has time, when he isn't in the middle of running from one side of the ship to another to detect a breakdown, when he's calmer.

When he's less afraid.

## XV

While everyone is preparing for the evening meal, she decides to go down to the engine room to reassure, in turn, those who weren't able to hear her in the wardroom, to show them that she hasn't forgotten them, and also to find out what role each of them is playing in the complex marriage of fuel and fire. She wears coveralls like her sailors, slips on protective goggles, and heads down to the boiler.

She greets each man she meets, but cannot, amid the din, reprise her long speech. She hopes her smile will suffice, the controlled assertion of this smile, of this gaze—never flinching or vague—which is her strength and which puts her at ease in giving instructions to each group.

—

"We may have found the source of the breakdown, captain," the chief engineer shouts in her ear. "We still need to confirm, but it seems that it's coming from the pump, a slowing down of the pump. We'd need to disassemble it to examine where it got bogged down and then proceed with a thorough cleaning; but to do that we'd need some time, to stop over at a port for several days."

She asks:

"Do you think we can carry on like this until our destination?"

"Hard to say," he shouts. "There's the risk that something else breaks down suddenly, and then nothing would work."

So, it's the pump. The big, red heart. The huge piece of flesh is tired of ferrying all that blood, of pumping for everyone. Or of moving forward, from mist to warm rain. Or of bleeding, amid total indifference.

How to help you, animal? How to make it possible for you to rest? How to begin communicating with your relentlessly pulsing machine logic and earn your acceptance when we are only parasites, when we pretend—with the greatest faith in the world—to orient ourselves using bits of colored paper, to know where our journeys lead?

—

"Let's keep going. When we're out of the mist, we can stop the engines again and begin the repairs."

"Very well, captain. But what if something breaks down first?"

"I'll take the responsibility."

"Without any disrespect, I know engines . . ."

"This one I know, too, believe me. I'm getting to know it better and better."

When the rain stops, something about this day will have become clarified. Everyone's thoughts will find their equilibrium again. She can't waste her time explaining to the crew. She knows, and that's enough. And it's enough, too, to feel the ship cleaving the water, to feel the rain beating against the windows, to feel the calm with which, in spite of it all, everyone has gone back to work. The slight slowness in her has turned into curiosity, into a tranquil progression toward the next discovery. It's enough to know that the white of the cloud that enveloped them, at least until now, hid them from others' sight. It's helped them delay this arrival, and the next departure, and the return, and the departure, and all this absurd coming and going until the day they retire, when they'll have to gaze at the water from a bench by the shore.

Drenched with sweat in her coveralls, she goes from one station to another to ask a few more questions, give news of her firm decisions. She makes the rounds and inspects the tools: the giant wrenches and all the different pliers they need to adjust the tanks. She understands something global, even without having learned it—a logic specific to the machine—and forgets it immediately. Though it's as beautiful as the law of wind in sails.

It seems to her that she's spread a little calm amid the workmen's agitation, that she's made the problem seem a little less serious. She watches each of them return to his task with a more confident step. Everything begins to feel a little lighter.

Without knowing how it happened—was it a cigarette break, or had they gone to fetch a missing tool upstairs?—she finds herself alone in the engine room with its furnace-like heat. She lies down again and places her ear on the floor to listen. She's listening for the dissonance, the heart murmur. But what she hears is that steady, strong beating of an animal, that giant, calm pounding. So she places her hand on the floor and smiles.

On land, this would be like placing her arm around a horse's neck and breathing along with it. Waiting for trust to be born, that mute connection we believe to be loyalty, something eternal, when we know that everything begins again each day.

But it's harder, old girl, to tame whales.

Close your eyes. You are not responsible for all the hearts beating around you. Look at how well it's doing, the beast, and all the forces, the masses, the currents beneath it. Listen to the sailors' hearts, too, these portable pumps for grown men, and the batucada it is just to be together and alive. Listen to how each of them stirs, without even knowing it, each his own ocean. What life, old girl, on your little ship. You can be proud. What life.

And while she's there, stretched out in the grease, cheek against the metal, in her coveralls that are a little too big, she feels light and likely more unearthly than ever in body and spirit, certain that nothing bad will happen if only she asks herself the right questions, certain that the ship's heart will keep beating in unison with her own for as long as she wills it.

"There are strange things, many strange things happening on this ship."

Without lifting her head, she knows exactly who has spoken. The blond boy is a few meters behind her.

"You say this because I have an ear glued to the floor?"

"Not only."

She remains prone. All she has to do is sense his presence, imagine how he's holding onto the guardrail, how he's looking all around him, not quite entering the room, preferring to stay always at the edge of the frame.

She hopes that if she doesn't move, he'll be quiet. She doesn't need his opinion, doesn't need him diagnosing her way of embracing the ship and trusting it. She listens to him breathing, he too, echoing the ship. She tries to isolate his heartbeat but can't. Only silence emanates from him. He continues, his voice almost pleasant, when one isn't frozen by the transparency of his eyes.

"There's this freighter, drifting, not knowing why it goes."

"You mean 'where it goes'?"

"No, I mean why it goes."

"I've got things under control. I'm used to this—"

She doesn't have time to finish her sentence.

"No. No one is used to drifting."

She waits for him to add something, but he doesn't. Or it's lost in the screeching of pistons.

*You have no heart* is the only thing she would want to tell him before he leaves, certain to have seen through him, but she's aware of the grandiloquence of the statement and immediately takes back this impossible assessment. Another sentence for the black book.

If she can't hear his heart, she does recognize the squeaking of his shoes: his body exists, then. Their inopportune squeaking continues until he leaves the room. The door shuts too heavily for her to remain in her floating state. So the captain contents herself with closing her eyes, preparing herself slowly for the idea of getting to her feet; but the whale brings her back to its purring, and the abyss to its obscurity.

"Captain, is everything OK?"

A man is leaning over her. Opening her eyes, she recognizes the chief mate and smiles at the hurried way he props her up, makes sure she isn't injured.

"Thank you, it's nothing, it's the heat: I'm not as used to it as the engineers are. Everything is OK. Everything is really OK. Help me get up. I'll drink some water, I'll get some fresh air."

"Maybe you should rest. Today has been a long day."

## XVI

They used to make sacrifices so that the fleets would set sail again. To prevent the moment when the soldiers suddenly went mad. To start up the winds, they led little girls to the altar—instead of lambs. They told themselves that it must be a god thing and a question of clemency to be implored, and that a young girl, as long as she was dressed in white, as long as she had long hair and lace undergarments, yes, a young girl should do the trick to wake the winds and set off again for war and navigation. That's what she read in the tragedies when she was in high school. Without understanding what could possibly link this land-bound girl with the soldiers stuck over there. Without understanding that everything always had to be resolved through men's great violence. She saw herself as Iphigenia, breaking her chains, climbing aboard the ships instead of onto the sacrificial mount, and putting herself to work steering them, these clumsy crews, to victory if that's what they wished, or else toward the reasoning that would cool their rage.

Today it's her own ship that refuses to budge, when there's no reason to rely on nature, when the winds, when the gods, when the crosscurrents have long been mastered or massacred. After all, we use engines to propel ourselves into space, so crossing the smallest ocean . . .

What will we sacrifice, boat? What will we throw into the sea to make you come back to our side?

Maybe it would have been enough for them to wait, motionless, each in his puddle, for no wars to ever happen, for Iphigenia to age in her anonymity and boredom.

Now it's a pitch-black, starless night. No moon. Nothing. A vast shield of clouds. A black night over black water that doesn't even remember that it rained, and for comfort there is only the yellow light of electric bulbs. Somewhere in this yellowness, the men are playing cards, are snoozing, headphones over their ears, are drinking, are laughing or clenching their teeth. But they keep the electric light on in this total darkness. They let themselves go, down to the bodies curled into a ball on the bunk, lost in a movie or in a half-sleep brought on by the swaying.

It's the little cabin in fairy tales, the glow in the forest clearing. And the clearing itself is poised on a nutshell, and the whole thing floats on a stream before reaching the sea. And even should there be wind or pummeling, should the surrounding forest or the ocean become black, infinite, and menacing, here inside, as long as the yellow light survives, there will always be the magic of the hearth, this sense of security. She always believed you needed a storm to appreciate the little cabin buffeted by winds, to turn it into a cocoon. But the dark, calm night and the rain that lights can't pierce are nice, too.

On the bridge, she lets herself be rocked. She continues to note the ship's position, every twenty minutes a cross on the punctured sheet. The points are closer and closer together. They're slowing down. They're settling in.

She communicates regularly with the chief engineer, who didn't want to go to bed either, who is carrying out his investigation of the gauges and engines with increasingly obvious excitement.

———

"Captain, it appears that the pump is adjusting its tempo, that it's playing, to make . . . to make, don't take me for a madman, to make a kind of music. Captain, do you copy?"

"I don't take you for a madman."

"A regular rhythm that changes every once in a while. What's incredible is that it doesn't always slow down. If it were a system failure, it would simply slow. But here, no: sometimes it speeds up, too. For a few minutes, we pick up speed. Then it calms down again. As if it's going to sleep."

"That's what I think, too."

"Captain, I have the feeling that it isn't mechanical. Everything's working, the pump works, that's for sure."

"That's what I think, too."

"My theory, captain, is that there's been a very complex electronic malfunction. We've shifted into manual mode, but there must be something resisting. Like . . . Have you heard the story about the two artificial intelligences that managed to communicate with each other in a language that humans can't understand?"

"No, tell me."

A short silence on the radio transmitter. Time enough for a smile on either end, for a clearing of the throat.

—

"Recently, two computers managed to exchange some information, rendering it unintelligible for humans or other computers. Encoding it, in a way. No one has any idea what they told each other. It opens up many possibilities . . ."

"Do you . . . No, nothing."

"Yes, captain, go ahead?"

"Do you think it's possible that our ship . . . that our ship has developed a sort of autonomy, a personality of its own?"

Silence again. Words weighed on either end.

"I think, captain, that that would be a slightly romantic vision. That we should perhaps instead believe that it's a system malfunction after the unplanned hiatus this morning."

She struggles to contain her exaltation, her sudden passion, nascent and immediate, for these artificial intelligences, for this ship and its metal logic, for everything that suddenly manages to seize its independence and give no explanation. She bursts out laughing, and it's her way of crying out her love for everything that won't let itself be decoded, everything that decides to make its own poetry while no one is watching—and who cares if it's a path filled with pain, and who cares if there's death in the end.

When her father came back from his last expedition, several years before she'd chased after him in the rain, he didn't speak. Only in the final months did he start to use a few basic words, no doubt essentially so he'd be left alone.

Within the family, this mutism, this form of separation, had been unacceptable. It was soon diagnosed as dementia, but for her that's not what it was. Her family members would have had to know how to listen to the silence and not punish as quickly as possible what they took to be contempt. She, too, of course, was hurt that he had not made her a confidante in this thing he must have gone through and that didn't concern land-dwellers but should have concerned her, his sailor daughter, apprentice officer who was just beginning to understand what they were, these great stupors that can seize you when land is no longer in sight. She had tried to find auspicious moments, to go on long walks with him near the water, then far from the water, and she had waited hours for his aphasia to reveal something. He had said nothing. Bitterness had turned to understanding, to a strange intimacy with his old-man secrets.

She had continued to move forward with her intuitions and for several weeks that had been enough to rebuild a kind of strained, shifting bond between her and the captain without a ship. Among her clearest apparitions was that of the face of death, which her father had certainly seen in a way one never should in one's life, and which explained his silences better than any scans he was subjected to. She thought of the passage in the Odyssey that had struck her when she was young. Ulysses, lost at sea, accidentally approaches the kingdom of the dead and goes on to visit them. He sees the recently lost sailors, comrades he didn't know had died, and finally—dramatic welling of tears—his mother. He is the only being in the world to whom this chance is granted of speaking with her one last time. Perhaps her father, too, found Ulysses's secret passage, but instead of returning home along the path, stayed there, in this world between worlds, where it matters little if you walk in the rain or look at a wall for hours on end until your own death, finally.

When she goes out to breathe in the nighttime, the chief mate takes his turn studying the map. He knows this course, calculated to be the fastest, by heart. A route along which dozens of merchant ships cross paths each day. A route for exchanging metal boxes between the two sides of the Atlantic and creating needs among those who won't have the means to satisfy them. A route like a net. Do other sailors ask themselves, as he does, the same questions almost daily: how do we get out? How do we not get trapped? How do we keep making a living from the sea and from these journeys without selling or buying anything? Maybe that's what they're doing in spite of themselves. By slowing down the rhythm. By not rendering accounts. By not fulfilling the objectives.

He turns the smooth little stone over in his pocket, then places it on the map, a few centimeters from the hole she pierced, and suddenly it's an island appearing in the Atlantic. A round island, reassuring, uninhabited. A little pocket island, but vast relative to the map's scale, a new continent, round and gray, that needs only to be filled in with relief and color. So he moves the rock off the work table and, with the pencil they use to mark their location, draws a deviant line, at an angle from their route, then a new island, still unnamed, with an inlet drawn for docking, some mountainous heights, the necessary water, forest, and beaches sheltered from the wind.

And from the swimming spot pierced in the paper to this new land he's just invented for them are barely a few hours of drifting for the ship. A harbor, he thinks: a refuge that's easy to reach by early morning.

All around, he makes the mist dissipate into small gray patches that thin out. Just a little curtain to manage the sight of land. Just some wrapping paper so he can offer his comrades the joy of this territory expressly imagined for them.

And they won't build any permanent houses. Everyone will just be stopping by.

On the freighter he draws next, tiny between two points but wholly turned toward this new shore, he traces a big open eye in place of the name, with fine eyelashes, a translucent iris.

When he's finished his drawing—careful, precise— he takes the eraser to make the paper suitable for work again, a measuring tool with immutable reference points. Then changes his mind. Leaves the mark of his passage, his little childishness, his tiny moment of dissidence.

# XVII

This is where she hid, too, at first, when she didn't want to be found. Now, when she needs to, she manages to hide inside herself without letting it show. She pushes the door to this dark room, a little-used gym that manages to squeeze in a few weight lifting machines, several barbells on the floor, and spare tracksuits. Not surprisingly, a smell of sweat floats on the air, and most certainly always will.

She has come to the conclusion that if anyone is hiding on the ship it must be here, in this gym.

"Is anyone here? Is this where you sleep? I know you're here; I can hear you breathing."

It's not true. All she can hear is her heart and no other beating yet that might confirm another's presence. But it's not impossible that a man could be lying on the floor: the equipment left there casts shadows that could be a curled-up silhouette, a slumped body awaiting only the arrival at port to end this absurd situation.

"Are you going to the West Indies? A stowaway for the West Indies? Usually people are looking to go the other way. You know, it won't be easy to leave the port. You've been lucky so far. Very lucky. I must not have been in my right mind to have let this happen."

She doesn't come any closer. She doesn't turn on the light. She doesn't attempt any movement that might shift her point of view on the mass of shadows before her, that might reveal that she's speaking to a mere motionless pile of tarps and ropes.

"I know how to hear things that few people hear—the sound of breathing few people would notice. It's a family trait. But you're better at this game than I am. You'll just have to be careful with your shoes."

No tremor, still, just the strange echo of her own voice.

"Are you a sailor, too? You know what I mean by sailor. I'm not talking about a profession or career. But that other thing. I think you are. A sailor. Rejected by the land."

—

Still no sound save the nighttime preparations all around her: the last nightcap in one of the common areas, the end of a movie, the shower, and the smoke unfurling from a last cigarette that masks for a second or two the insistent brightness of the stars. Still, she continues her monologue before the wall in front of her; she trusts her intuition and her knowledge of the comings and goings on her ship.

"You can't stay here. Take one of the empty cabins, the ones on the first floor, I'll put your situation in order. Yes. That's what I'll do and end this day and night on a high note: I'll sit at the computer, the one that links us to the rest of the world for a few hours each day, and I'll set things in order. I'll pen some mail and sign some papers and vouch for the truth and use my authority and it'll be the most relaxing thing I've done these last few weeks, setting all this in order, and I'll disembark in Guadeloupe as planned and change freighters if this one isn't running and sleep twenty or so hours in a hotel on firm ground, which will continue to sway until my body gets used to it, and leave rested and take up work again for the years I have left to fulfill my job. Have you got your papers with you? I'll create a new file for you right away. You must have a photo lying around. We'll figure out the medical certificate, the birth certificate later on. Your identification card will be enough. Will you give it to me, please? You must have it in your wallet, at the bottom of a suitcase. We always have those things on hand.

"Okay. Come on now.

"I know you're not staying in one of the cabins, I've finished checking the names and faces of all the occupants. You can get up now."

Of course, since she's already speaking on supposition, since she's already letting her words bounce off the gym walls, she can go further—no modesty holding her back—and tell him about her current intuition, so precise that she herself doesn't call it intuition but files it away mentally in another notebook, the one that holds the things about which she's certain, but that simply aren't ripe enough to be shared. Unless, as she often tells herself, the problem is actually the world's maturity, always slightly behind the flow of her thoughts.

"We know each other, don't we? You and I, we've met before, right? I can't remember where or when anymore, can't be certain of the notion without all my thoughts taking on strange colors, but it'll come back to me. Yes, from one second to the next, something will come back to me, something will cross the night and take advantage of a slightly higher wave to splash right in my face. Isn't that how things are supposed to happen? A little detail, a smell, a color, a type of silence, and everything will come back at once, and I'll know who you are and what you're doing on my freighter. I'm waiting. The satisfaction of completing the puzzle, of placing that last piece we merely have to put down and it slides flush with the others all on its own. Yes, what relief it'll be in a few seconds, when I put together the puzzle of your face. If you show yourself, I'm sure I'll be able to recognize something and it will all come back like a déjà vu."

Usually, it's names she chases after, hunting down lost first names by going through the alphabet in her head; but she doesn't have an alphabet for faces, nor for memories she might have had. She may be skilled at waiting, at deciphering each clue in atmospheric changes, but in the last few months her invisible investigations have been increasingly left unresolved.

"The older I get, the faster what escapes me glides and slips between my fingers."

———

To the very end, she awaited a sign in the little house at the edge of the sea. No longer any explanation, really, but at least some encouragement. A gesture in her direction before his death.

But maybe the silence was the response. A way of forcing her to let go of any need for approval. It's this way that she'll have to continue to navigate, to move forward both her freighter and her several-ton-heavy heart.

Three weeks before the departure, when she'd arrived at her father's house, there was a small blue car parked in the courtyard. She recognized the nurse's car, but he was supposed to come much earlier—why was he still here, why this feeling that he was waiting for her on the doorstep instead of having left her instructions, as on previous days, and the confirmation of his next visit scribbled on a Post-it?

Why the pale face?

She walked through the courtyard and the nurse was leaning against the doorjamb, on the edge of a scene that was already forming in slow motion in her head, because she understood very well what this presence meant and because, therefore, she'd immediately entered the mode of recording everything, of decoding anything that could prove or disprove what she had already absorbed anyway as soon as the blue car appeared in her field of vision, and this pale-faced nurse at the edge of the frame.

"I don't know which one of you has the other's face."

In her mental recording, there is the blinding light and the too-pale eyes of the nurse, and something that doesn't fit the scene, maybe the shouts of children a few streets away, or a gaping trash can that wasn't brought in and strips the scene of its gravity, or simply this stranger to the house, who leans against it, impassive.

"I know what you have to tell me. Give me time to make my way up the walkway to you. Give me a few seconds before the annihilating blast."

And then time took on its consistency again: trivial acceleration of the conversation, street sounds, and the blue car's engine starting up again after the murmured condolences, after evoking the long list of procedures, the claims, the documents, the matters of custom.

She doesn't remember the hours that followed, aside from the fact that she stayed sitting on the front steps for a long time and packed her bag hastily—she never brought much when she visited, no need for frills and nothing to do but be present—looking at nothing around her in order to trick herself into thinking she was already gone, to keep as few memories as possible of this house.

"Come out now, please. I'd simply like to go to sleep. I think tonight I'll finally be able to."

So she moves her hand toward the light switch and holds her breath as the whitish neon lights blink on, haltingly, in the gym.

The black mass gradually reveals itself, a heap of tracksuits, a stash of buoys and a few lamps.

Some empty bottles and a still-smoking cigarette butt, signs of a recent presence.

# XVIII

He hates having to do this. Every time, it's the thing that could make him stay on land: having to take on the medical responsibilities, making every effort possible to remember how to patch up injuries according to first-aid protocol (though he reviews it once a year during a mandatory workshop that makes him sick to his stomach), observing as diligently as he can so as not to let a single symptom escape detection when a sailor comes to the infirmary.

The chief mate is on call in the tiny cabin that serves as a pharmacy and medical examination room, and it's she, the captain, who is lying on the stretcher. He was awakened early in the night by loud knocking at his door, by a sailor who had found her passed out in the corridors. The two of them carried her here and then he closed the door, stayed alone with her. It didn't take long for her to come to again, to smile at him.

"Sorry."

On top of it all, the ship is pitching; the calm sea is a thing of the past. The chief mate wonders what they're crossing for the waves to be so high again, which is in no way improving the comfort of the situation. But they're moving forward, no? Aren't they moving forward once again?

He takes her blood pressure, notes that she's conscious, weak but conscious. He asks the usual questions to gauge her confusion and it's not as bad as he expected.

"Can I get up?"

"It would be great if we could understand what these were, these fainting spells. Why since this morning we've regularly found you lying on the ground everywhere all over the ship."

"You're exaggerating a bit, no?"

"I'm lightening the mood. But seriously. I'm following protocol. I called a doctor on the emergency hotline and—I know you're discreet about your private life, and it's none of my business—they're asking me to ask you . . ."

"I'm not pregnant."

"OK, OK. It's noted, I just had to rule out that possibility . . ."

"You're making me laugh."

"Why?"

"You're blushing."

"Try to put yourself in my shoes."

"I've been there. Undressing men, patching them up, comforting them."

"But there was less risk that they were . . ."

"Pregnant."

"Pregnant."

"It's true. Thank you."

"For what?"

"For being concerned about me. I'll be fine. I think my body will be fine, and my head, we'll say it's known worse."

"Do you want a little pill? I have some good stuff on hand."

"Whisky?"

"Yes, that too. Upstairs."

"Shall we go up and see what's happening?"

She moves to get up, feels it coming over her again: the desire to survey her little world, to go back and check each spot with her fingertips before returning to align herself with the prow, before fixing her eyes on the horizon again.

"Wait, wait. Don't you want to stay here and rest a little longer?"

"I'm telling you, I feel better."

"At least give me a chance to play my role fully, I'm beginning to enjoy it. Seriously. Let yourself go."

"What are you doing?"

"Hold on."

Gently, he places his hands on her shoulders. Real bricks, as he suspected. He slides his thumbs under her shoulder blades and begins slowly to massage her.

"You're going to have to let yourself be taken care of a little. I contacted the medical team at the hospital. As soon as we land at Point-à-Pitre, they'll carry out all the medical exams possible. It would be good for you to stay on land a little while. Enough time to figure out where your fainting spells are coming from."

"I'm telling you, I'm fine. My body. My body is fine."

As he speaks, he keeps moving his thumbs. He's not sure how well-founded his initiative is: there's more tension than he'd expected and—but too late, now that he's started—it's no doubt totally out of place, this massage, this almost-tenderness, whereas for years the slightest amicable gesture has been scrutinized . . . for fear of what? A door that would open to awkwardness, a slippery slope, a universe so vast that it would swallow him immediately. Yes, that's it, he would be sucked into space and its infinite void.

"Thank you. That helps, thank you."

"What are you holding onto, what are you refusing to relax, here, for the rubber band to be so tight?"

"What rubber band?"

"Between here and here."

He keeps one hand on her shoulder and, slowly, places the other on her stomach.

"It's as if you needed a rubber band pulled tighter and tighter in order to stand up."

"Hey there, you're reading me like an open book."

"Breathe instead of mocking me."

"Do you think the world would keep turning without my legendary rigidity?"

"I doubt it, but you could try."

—

An hour later, they're still in each other's arms. A miracle of the ocean: she surprised herself by crying all of a sudden, without any preparatory sadness, almost joyfully, and now she mops up the hiccups, the flood of tears and snot with tissues he continually hands to her. Each new bout of sobs opens up new waterways, a trough unthinkable just minutes before; it's streaming on either side of her nose, all the way to her chin, and in a dash to the ear as soon as she turns her head a little. He maneuvers now around the flooded face, brushes aside her hair, hands her another tissue, notes the spreading redness, kisses her nose and forehead, kisses her mouth, and he must be crying a bit too, since his eyelashes are wet and his cheeks red. But he's held fast, he can be proud; now, he can aspire to any rank. He bailed them out as he should: soon there will be almost no trace of the fault lines, only a face lying on his shoulder, dry and restful, a face weary from the crossing but victorious, just a few traces of salt in the nascent wrinkles. Good work, honestly. It's sparkling now, this face, if you look closely; it almost seems to be smiling, calmly beached on this shoulder—why leave again for another voyage?

"Is it already morning?"

"The sun rises early in these parts."

"Will you allow me to return to my station?"

"You're in charge."

"Do you feel that rumbling?"

"What is it?"

"We've picked up speed."

# XIX

"Allow me to inform you that no artificial intelligence could create a horizon like that," says the chief engineer, smiling, having joined the crowd around the map on the bridge.

"Very funny, thank you."

"So?"

"There's no question. The GPS is clear. And all the measurements confirm it. We're arriving."

"Is that La Désirade?"

"The island itself, you'd better believe it."

Of course it's she, in the foreground when you're coming from old Europe, solid as relief. They say it's the first bit of land Christopher Columbus's men spotted after their stopover in the Canary Islands. *O, much-desired land*, they are said to have sighed, sailors to the core yet still yearning for the security of a rock if it could give them some landmarks in space and time. She sees the men who make up her company leaning over the railings, they, too, outstretched in this desire for sand and limestone.

She isn't sure if she shares this desire for land, not yet, not without having prepared herself. But relief, yes. Once the unloading is done, the end of the voyage will mean the beginning of several days in the archipelago, walking through the wilder vegetation to the top of the volcano.

So here is the new horizon. All the more gripping because they weren't expecting it any longer. All the gaze has to do to get lost in it is jump over the red and blue containers, which stand always in their neat rows, with the inscriptions they don't even think to read anymore, since they see them every morning. They'd forgotten about these big metal boxes—the whole reason for each journey, but once on the water, the sailors don't give them a second thought. The boxes only remind them, on some days, of the graceless century to which they all still belong.

Now the sailors are spread out on the ship, alone or in twos or threes. Those who are near each other speak in signs and onomatopoeias. They've crossed over to the other side of language.

Sailing at full speed, they rediscover their bodies. Twenty bodies standing taut, at work. They'd constructed a balance—the balance of an entire life—and a slight change in speed set everything swaying. In recovering the once-familiar sensations, they think of those women and men who are sent into space, of the parenthesis of lightness it must be to feel weightless, untethered. Ageless in the slowed-down time. But they also know the violence of the return, the accelerated aging that causes everything you've tried to avoid to suddenly catch up with you.

Today, for them, it's much the same: all of the suspended hours come to lodge themselves in the ache of their necks and the creases of their faces. They've paid off all their debts to time's passing.

As they near the strip of land, she regains her consciousness of weights, measurements, the cargo to be lifted and the price of merchandise that peaks or plummets according to laws that have little to do with the sea. At port, she'll become the vehicle for information and foodstuffs and, surprisingly, the one who speaks louder than everyone else.

From up on the bridge, she mentally re-counts the men around her who can no longer pry their eyes from the land in sight. They are twenty. She knows now that she won't search the ship for the last one. As long as she can see beyond the engines, to the buried heart beating its reconciled rhythm, she knows that all is well. She breathes.

Suddenly, the smell of trees reaches them.

And those birds, whose cries and impatience they'd forgotten.

The landscape is becoming clearer, and each sailor is accelerating. The decibels rise to the level she recognizes as they ready themselves to arrive at port. Each man summons his memory of docking and his knowledge of coasts. What they need now is to prepare for their return to speech, overwhelming and constant, to the shouts at the market, to the words that jostle in mouths to tell them all at once the news of this place since the last time. They have to become once again beings free to move about on paths, in cars.

And, as soon as this evening, they'll dance.

As for her, she'll swim at the foot of a waterfall, will put her head under the icy, turquoise water; it'll be her turn to be naked in the water, alone in the world in this setting that mirrors the paradise of books and paintings.

And, all through the night, the birds will yell and fall silent in the morning: a world upside down.

"What are you thinking about?"

"About the paths I'll have to find again, between the trees."

"You're not going to go home?"

"I'll stay here for a little while. And you?"

The chief mate hasn't had time to ask himself the question. For several days he's forgotten that dates and airplanes existed.

Marie-Galante appears now, eternally round.

"For the first time in my life, I have no idea."

## ACKNOWLEDGMENTS

*Ultramarine* was born during a writer's residency aboard the CMA-CGM cargo ship *Fort Saint-Pierre* in August 2012, organized by the Centre nationale du théâtre on the initiative of Laurent Lalanne. I warmly thank them.

Thanks also to Stéphane Beauvois, the ship's captain, for his time and for the enthusiasm with which he welcomed me and those who were also on board for the trip: the writers Claudine Galea, Magali Mougel, Éric Pessan, Sabine Revillet, and Michel Sidoroff.

I continued the writing at the Maison de la poésie in Rennes in fall 2016.

Finally, I would like to thank Philippe Malone, Antoine Mouton, and Benoît Reiss for their guidance and kindness.

Mariette Navarro is an educator, novelist, and dramaturg. She has been part of the Comédie de Béthune since 2014. She was also associated with the Scènes du Jura for the 2015–2016 season and the théâtre de l'Aquarium for the 2017–2018 season. Since 2016, she has co-directed the Grands fonds collection with Cheyne éditeur. Her plays include *Nous les vagues* followed by *Célébrations* (Quartett, 2011), *Prodiges*® (Quartett, 2012), *Les Feux de poitrine* (Quartett, 2015), *Les Chemins contraires* (Cheyne éditeur, 2016), *Zone à* étendre (Quartett, 2018), *Les Hérétiques* (Quartett, 2018), and *Les Désordres imaginaires* (Quartett, 2020). Her novella *Alors Carcasse* (Cheyne éditeur, 2011) won the Robert-Walser Prize 2012. *Ultramarine* is her first novel.

Eve Hill-Agnus is a Franco-American writer, editor, and translator. This is her first novel-length translation.